RAPTURE

YOGENDRA NIKALE

Copyright © Yogendra Nikale
All Rights Reserved.

This book has been published with all efforts taken to make the material error-free after the consent of the author. However, the author and the publisher do not assume and hereby disclaim any liability to any party for any loss, damage, or disruption caused by errors or omissions, whether such errors or omissions result from negligence, accident, or any other cause.

While every effort has been made to avoid any mistake or omission, this publication is being sold on the condition and understanding that neither the author nor the publishers or printers would be liable in any manner to any person by reason of any mistake or omission in this publication or for any action taken or omitted to be taken or advice rendered or accepted on the basis of this work. For any defect in printing or binding the publishers will be liable only to replace the defective copy by another copy of this work then available.

Mother was cooking in the kitchen 2 hours before sunset and 8-year-old Michael entered inside the kitchen in stealth mode for the pastries kept in the oven. Michael watches Mom was busy cooking and it was an opportune moment. So he removes 2 pastries from the oven and keeps them on a plate without making a sound, as his mother was staring at him.

Michael gets scared watching her gaze, "Oh god! Mom, you scared me."

Mom replies, "That's our dessert after dinner."

Michael answers that it's still time for dinner and he is hungry already.

Mother asks sarcastically to take the meatballs and pasta and avoid taking the pastry.

Michael replies, "Come on maa do you really think i am gonna have anything else when the oven is hot. Everyone loves your pastries"

Mother tells, " Come on go now run and don't fill yourself. I see 2 of them."

Michael runs out of the house screaming, "The other one is not for me Maa"

Mother smiles and gets back to cooking because she knows where Michael is headed.

Michael took the pastries to his neighbor Veronica . They both are of the same age. She was waiting on their building terrace.

Veronica watching Michael enter, "What took you so long?"

Michael explains, " Mom caught me stealing, I was too scared, thought she might hit me. Please don't make me steal stuff."

Veronica replies "Stealing from our own house is not stealing."

Veronica doesn't waste a single second and starts eating and she finishes the cake before Michael does.

Veronica starts licking her fingers, "Marvelous! Mike seriously no one beats the taste of your mother's pastries."

Michael offers Veronica his cake but she says, "No I'm full" and burps. Michael reacts to her burp, "Well that's a singer's voice." and they both start laughing.

Veronica says," No kidding. When I will be a big singer, I will keep your Mom with me. and all day I will eat pastries."

Michael replies, "Mom says too much sweet will rot your teeth."

Veronica

"Who cares about teeth sooner or later they are Gonna fall."

Michael

" If you take my Mom with you, what will happen to me? Where will I go."

Veronica

" You also stay with us but you need to work ok, my father doesn't work. He gets drunk every day after my mother died, he shouts and yells in the house. I don't want you to be like him."

Michael

" But what should I do, I don't even know how to sing."

Veronica

" There are many things to do in life. Let me think about you. Hmm, you be a boss man. "

Michael

" What is that?"

Veronica

" Boss man is like giving orders to everyone, they don't work much but their only job is to give orders and that's easy. You be a boss man or you are not welcomed in my house."

Suddenly they both hear glass break sound and they look down at the street. There were 3 teenage boys coming out of a window of a house across the street and they ran like hell from there.

Michael

" What are these guys up to now?"

Veronica
" You know them."
Michael
" Yeah they snatch money from all the children in school. I wonder what they have done now."
Veronica
" Let's check out."
Michael
" No Veron, they might catch us. I'm not coming with you."
Veronica forces Michael and he decides to go with her to see what those boys are upto and Michael has seen them many times near the abandoned factory. So they decided to sneak into the place.
Michael and Veronica reached the spot and were looking inside the factory from a window glass. The factory was burned many years ago and so was the window, the window glass was turned black. It was not clear what those robbers were doing inside. They can hear them but they can't see.
Michael in fear, " Veron we shouldn't be here, lets go from here."
Veronica
" Relax, what are they doing?"
Michael
"I don't know i am not getting a clear view."
Veronica looks around and finds a way in through the broken ventilator and she forces Michael to get in and see what's happening inside.
Michael
" I am not Goanna do that."
Veronica
" If you won't do it, I will never speak with you again. "
So Michael decides to enter the demon's pit. He enters and watches them from the holes of the old rusty broken vent. The robbers were

counting money. A guy named Bosco had a big scar on his face, a black guy named Nathan and a fair guy named Edward were having a conversation.

Edward

" We are still short for one beer."

Bosco to Edward

" Maybe you don't drink today. Call it a day off "

Edward

" Why me ? Why don't you ask Nathan ."

Nathan

" No way man, I can't sleep without trippin."

Suddenly the broken vent falls down and Michael with it. Veronica runs away from the spot watching him fall inside the factory. The sudden bang shook the robbers. And they saw a broken vent on the floor and a child coming out of it. Bosco signs Edward to catch the kid. Edward runs towards Michael and grabs the back of his neck and makes him stand.

Edward

"You little rat, what were you looking at?"

Edward brings Michael towards his partners holding his neck. Michael struggled to get out of Edward's hands but he couldn't.

Edward

" We got a peeping tom over here guys."

Michael's struggle to escape agitated Nathan . So Nathan slapped him and Michael was still trying to escape.

Bosco watching Michael.

" You got fighting spirit kid."

Bosco orders his partners to check his pocket. Nathan and Edward start checking Michael's pocket, he was not letting them do that but he couldn't stop the robbers from checking him. Edward replies he has no bug on him.

Bosco to Michael

" Didn't your mama give you a penny for a candy today"

Michael stares at him in anger. Bosco sarcastically, "oh my god you are scaring me."

Nathan

" What do we do with this kid? He saw our spot, he might come with Cops if we let him go."

Bosco

" Throw him in the lake."

Edward

" Bosco , we can't do that. he is just a kid."

Nathan to Edward

" This kid will put us in prison. Do you want that? "

Edward looks at Michael in pity.

Edward

" Bosco , there might be some other way. "

Bosco

"Blind him, remove his eyes."

Michael speaks," Is your name Bosco ."

Bosco comes closer to the kid

" Why did you ask my name, is there anyone looking for me?"

Michael

" No."

Bosco

" So why did you ask?"

Nathan twisted his ears.

" Answer you little sheat."

Michael

" Even I want to be a boss when I grow up, that's why?"

Bosco laughs.

Edward

" He is not our boss, his name is Bosco . "

Bosco

" Alright leave him, let him be. "

Nathan

" But?"

Bosco stares at Nathan for a second . Edward and Nathan leave Michael.

Bosco

" It's not easy being a boss. you have to work hard, get trained for it."

Michael

" I'll do whatever it takes. anything for being a boss man."

Bosco leers for a second

" Well then let's find out."

At the sun set the gang takes Michael in front of a house and Bosco explains to Michael to help Nathan in stealing stuff from that house.

Nathan to Bosco

"Bosco, this is a mistake. He will get us caught. "

Bosco whispers to Nathan

" If anything goes wrong, ditch the boy and run. I will watch the street and signal if anyone comes."

Bosco to Michael

" This is your test boy, pass this and you are in."

Bosco removes a cloth from his pocket and gives it to Michael to hide his face. Michael starts covering his face and Edward removes a knife from his pocket and throws it towards Nathan and Nathan catches it.

Edward says, "Just in case, protect the boy."

Edward looks at Michael and feels bad for him. Nathan and Michael start walking towards the targeted house. Nathan mask's his face after getting closer to the window of the house.

Nathan threatens Michael with a knife, " If you make any sound I will just cut your throat and the last thing you will see is blood splashing

from your neck and the sealing of that house." and he puts the knife in his back pocket. Nathan opens the window and lifts Michael and helps him get into the house. Michael enters the house from the window and watches a radio on and there is no sign of anyone else. Nathan whispering from outside the window, " Do you see anyone?" Michael nods his head no. Nathan also enters the house.
Nathan starts looking into the house and picks a vase and gives it to Edward standing outside the window. Edward runs towards Bosco on the street and hands him the Vase and runs back towards the window to grab more stuff from them.
Nathan next goes for the radio. Picks it up and watches Michael is not there. Nathan whispered, "Hey boy where are you. " Nathan looked around and he couldn't find Michael . Nathan watches the kitchen, Michael is not there. Nathan then enters a room. A woman was taking shower, he could see her from the transparent glass and Michael was removing jewellery from the cupboard.
Nathan whispers
" What the fuck are you doing?"
Michael put the jewellery in his pocket and he was about to put the necklace.
Nathan whispers
" Wait, throw it here "
Michael throws the necklace towards Nathan and he catches it and starts watching the necklace closely to know it's for real gold.
Nathan whispers to Michael
" Come on that's enough."
Michael starts walking towards Nathan and Nathan keeps walking watching the gold piece in his hand and he doesn't see the vase on the floor and it gets kicked by his leg and breaks. The sound of the vase alerts the woman and she calls on his husband, "William is that you?"

Nathan

" Oh sheat, come on run."

They both run towards the window. Nathan climbs on the window and his knife falls inside the house and Nathan comes out and meets Edward.

Edward to Nathan

" Where is the boy?"

Nathan

" Leave him, he is a dead weight anyway."

Nathan runs towards Bosco and Edward stands outside the window watching inside the house. Michael was struggling to climb the window.

Edward from outside

" Come on boy, come on."

Michael climbs the window and William the owner of the house catches him from behind and pulls him back in the house.

William

" Why you little scoundrel."

Edward takes a step back in fear but he still stands there watching inside.

Bosco screams.

"Eddy lets get the fuck out of here."

Edward to Bosco

"Wait he is still inside."

Nathan to Bosco

" Leave him, he decides to get caught." And they make a run from there.

William starts slapping and beating Michael. Michael falls on the floor near the knife and he grabs it. As William comes closer Michael stabs him and runs from the window. Edward watches Michael come out and William comes by the window holding his bloody arm. Michael

and Edward run from there.
In that abandoned place everyone is happy and counting the stuff and watching jewellery.

Nathan

" This is some real sheat. I guess we don't have to steel for a week."

Edward

" For a week, i think for months."

Bosco

" This is all because of Michael. If you work this way one day I guarantee your gonna be the boss."

Suddenly they all hear the sound of a woman scream "Michael" the gang watches a lady coming closer to them and yelling for Michael. Bosco removes a knife from his pocket. Michael reacts watching his mother, " oh sheat mama." After listening to Michael Bosco keeps the knife back.

Michael's mother enters yelling

" Michael, I've been looking for you all around. Veronica told me you fell here. Why didn't you come home Michael?"

Nathan , Edward starts hiding the jewellery watching Michael's Mother. She starts searching Michaels body, " Are you hurt, did you get any injury."

Bosco

" No Mom we cached him."

Mom to Michael

"So why didn't you come home?"

Bosco

" We were about to drop him home. It looked like the kid lost his way back home."

Michaels Mom to Bosco

" Thank you so much."

Mom catches Michaels hand and starts dragging him out of the factory.

"I told you to come back home and dinner is ready. Why did you come so far, from now on no going out, no more terrace and no Veron. Play in the house as much you like."

While the Mom was speaking, Michael looked back and watched Bosco . And Bosco smiles and whispers, " You are the boss." Michael smiles back at Bosco.

15 Years later, 1990's Goa.

Nathan , Edward , Bosco and George playing cards and drinking in their card club. Bosco owns the club. George is the security guard in Bishop's casino. Everyone just kept on playing and raising money. They were playing the flash game. Edward asks for a show. Everyone from the table shows their cards and George wins. Bosco had the higher cards but he still throwed the card on the table as if he ran out of luck.

Nathan

" Every time this fucker wins. How do you do that?"

George

" I guess it's just my time." and laughs.

The croupier starts dealing with the cards again. And George starts to grab money from the pot.

Bosco

"George that's a lot of money you been taking home tonight."

George

" This money is peanuts. The real money I saw today was in the vault of a casino. Mountain of money, taller than me. There are half a dozen men just to count the money. Man this Bishop makes a big number every night."

Bosco

" What are you talking about?"

George

" I say we grab it and never work for our entire life. Tired of this security job."

Bosco

" If Bishop finds out your dead."

George

" Better die rich than living poor."

Edward

" Shall we play?"

George

" Of course, boy. I guess you are very desperate to lose more." and Laughs.

Nathan

" Bishop owns the town, Casinos, card clubs, Drugs, anyone who is gonna try to steal from him, should have trucks to transport the loot."

George

" And a army to get out alive,"

Everyone from the table stares at George.

George

" Whenever there is loot. All the hitmen from his clubs gather together and they hunt down the robbers. it's like a sport to them."

A man from another table starts fighting with the card dealer saying " 2 Aces back to back. You are cheating man, you are looting me."

Bosco watching them fight.

" fuck! Every time tourists over here they think they will gamble, win some money and get laid with an expensive hooker. Losing is also part of the game."

Bosco looks at the bar and screams, "Mike" Michael is sitting on a stool in front of the bar counter, he turns back and looks at Bosco. Michael is all grown up, strong and has a small pony tail at the back of his lower head.

Bosco to Michael

" Looks like we got a little problem."

Michael watches a guy fighting with a croupier. He turns back to the counter, takes a shot and lights his cigarette and gets up and walks near the table of trouble. Michael throws the smoke and grabs the guy who was fighting and takes him out of the card club.

George saw Michael taking the guy outside and he said, "Looks like the man lost his money, and now he is about to lose his jaw."

Michael takes the guy into a dark place outside the club.

The fighting man.

" Hey man, leave me, you guys are all thugs. What do you think you are doing here?"

Michael punches the man into his belly. The man bends down.

The man gets up in pain saying

"what the...."

Michael punches him in the face and the man falls down on the street. The man bleeds from his mouth and says, "Ohh man why are you beating me for?"

Michael sits down and looks at him. The man gets frightened.

Michael

" Look man, I got a job to do."

The fighting man

" But they are cheating."

Michael

" Who isn't? That's how it works, they make you win in the beginning and next they empty your pockets. How much did you loose?"

The fighting man

" A month's pay. "

Michael

" You got a wife? You married?"

The fighting man

" Yeah."

Michael

"Why did you come here in the first place? This is a dark world and you have a family. Go home, make love to your wife, buy her some gifts. Make a family. Wipe your face, look what you made me do?"

The fighting man wipes blood from his face.

"What am i gonna tell her?"

Michael removes the handkerchief and gives it to him.

" Take this for god sake, wipe that off. You are making me feel bad."

The fighting man wipes the blood from the cloth.

Michael

"Well this is what you got to do. Go home tell your wife that you got mugged on the street. Somehow you escaped. I bet she will understand. She will be happy that you are alive"

Man watches hin in fear

Michael

"And don't come back here again unless you wanna lose more. You got some money for cab."

The man replies, " No" then Michael removes money from his pocket and gives him, " here's some. Go home now, before you get into more trouble." Michael gets up and leaves from there.

The man watching Michael go, "Looks like the god has send a devil to do his work."

Inside the club Nathan asks George " What about the vault, is it breakable?"

George

" The vault is a piece of cake only if you have explosives. Without bombing it you may never enter."

Bosco asks, " What about the keys?"

George

" It's a big mystery over there. Every time the key guy changes. No one knows who has it."

Edward reacts " More the money, more the risk. "

George

" People who tried to steal from the Bishop went missing. Some say he has his own playground, men buried in it."

Michael enters inside the club and washes his hand at the basin and watching Michael Bosco said, " He is a powerful man I say. No one can ever beat such power."

George

" It's like putting your hand in the mamba's pit. We can only dream of looting him."

Nathan asks to show the cards, " Alright, lets see what you got."

Bosco has a higher card but he nods his head no to everyone. George wins again.

Edward

" This is some crock of sheat. Fucker wins again.."

George

" As i said before, it's my time."

Nathan , " I'm out man, tired of losing. Cant do anymore." And he gets up and walks towards the bar.

George

" Bosco, what about you? Are you playing ?"

Bosco

" Nah! I'm done for the night."

George replies, " Alright then, I ain't going empty handed." and he gets up and grabs the money and starts putting it in his pocket.

George saying goodbye, " Well i'll see you guys later." he also screams for Michael, "yo Mike, good bye."

Michael was standing near the bar counter and lighting his cigarette and he replies, " good bye George."

George

" Send my regards to your mother."
Nathan enters there with a drink, " Send my regards to you beautiful wife."
Edward and Nathan laughs and gives each other a fist bump.
George in anger, " Hey watch your mouth, don't you ever fucking go there."
Bosco to George
" Hey relax man."
Bosco in anger to Nathan
" Don't take it too far Nathan. "
Nathan
" Alright my bad forgive me."
George starts walking towards the exit.
Nathan to George
" Don't forget its your time."
George turns back, watches Nathan mumbles in anger and walks out of the door.
Nathan
" Maybe this Christmas you will catch me fucking your wife again."
Bosco is opening the bottle and making a drink.
Bosco
" Shut up will you?"
Nathan
" Come on, he is long gone. He cannot hear me. "
The exit is behind Bosco . Bosco asks Edward, " Is he ?"
Edward
" Yeah he is gone."
Bosco
" So we know now robing the casino is suicide mission."
Nathan
" My pockets are empty for what ? To know how we are gonna die"

Bosco

"Consider it as an investment. "

Edward

" How much did he even make tonight?"

Nathan

" Maybe 40k I guess."

Edward

" 40 grand, that fucker never would have seen such kind of money and for what ? Nothing. Getting into Bishop's vault is a way to hell, All waste."

Bosco

" At least we know now. When his place gets hit. All the hitmen from all his clubs gather together. "

Nathan

" So what difference does it makes?"

Bosco

" I got a plan, I just have to bring Rudy in."

Edward

" You mean that psychopath. He is a greedy dog."

Nathan

" After the loot he will kill us and grab the money."

Bosco

" I know this before you do but we are gonna need him."

Michael enters near the table wearing a jacket and Bosco stops talking about the heist.

Bosco

" Hey mickey need a drink?"

Michael

" Nah had enough, was about to hit the road."

Bosco

" That guy got too rough here. Did he leave or is he lying outside?

Don't tell me we got to bury him."

Michael gets seated on a chair.

" nah! taken care of, you won't see him again."

Bosco looks around and watches as there is no one in the club, " So no lamb to slaughter tonight. Well then, when you got to go then you got to go."

Edward

" Come on, what are you gonna do now? Lets have some drinkS and fuck some pussy."

Michael

" I have to reach somewhere, it's my girl's birthday. "

Bosco

" Hey Mike, give her my best wishes."

Nathan

"You got a girl? We never knew, you never brought her here."

Michael sarcastically answers, " Bring my girl here."

Edward

" Yeah man, that's right, never bring her here, she will leave you for good. Anyways congratulations and wish her from me"

Nathan also greets, "Congrats man."

Bosco

" Mike, I want to speak about something. There is a job."

Michael

" I figured, I saw a machine gun and a shotgun in the cabin. I think we are gonna hit big this time. But i ain't gonna kill no one."

Bosco

" The gun will be in your hand, you are the one gonna aim and pull the trigger. Don't blame us for that."

Michael says, " Can we stop this? We have enough already."

Bosco

" This is not the money I dreamed of. And you know you are free to make your own choice. If you want out then stay out. no one is forcing you."

Nathan , "But we may die without you Mike."

Michael stares at everyone's face in confusion

Bosco

" Ok, It's not today, don't worry. Go and celebrate your birthday. Forget about what's gonna happen. Just enjoy the night."

Michael gets up from the chair. Bosco reaches into his jacket and removes money and gives it to Michael.

Bosco

" And wait here's some money, buy her a good gift."

Nathan gets up with the bottle in his hand gives him saying, "And here it is, one for the road."

Everyone raises their glass and repeats after Nathan " One for the road."

Michael drinks from the bottle and keeps the bottle on the table. And everyone at the table drinks from their glass. Michael, "Good night fellas." and he walks out of there.

As Michael leaves Nathan asks Bosco, " Did you know he has a girl?"

Bosco

" No he never mentioned until today."

Edward

" That's called life, you should live it someday, Instead of banging other peoples wife."

Nathan

" Hey, that's real fun. No shame in it. I wonder what Michael is tapping tonight?"

Bosco

" Don't throw stones on a sleeping tiger. When he wakes up you might not have a place to run."

Nathan

" No, i am not thinking of taping his girl, it will spoil our brotherhood."

Bosco

" Nathan , I know you very well."

Everyone from the table starts laughing.

Bosco

" Alright, here's the plan. Now we know where the vault is located, don't we Nathan ?"

Nathan

" Yeah George 's wife gave me some instruction I made a map of it."

Edward asks, "Are you still tapping on her?"

Nathan, "Yeah whenever George has night shifts."

Bosco annoyingly

" Shall I proceed with the plan?"

Edward

"Yeah sorry man my bad."

Bosco

" I will hit the casino with Rudy and you guys stay outside the Irish club."

Nathan

"Irish is 3 miles from there. We will miss all the action."

Bosco explained the plan, " No you won't. As we hit the casino. The hitmen from the Irish club will head towards the casino and when they leave, you wait for 15 minutes outside and then hit the club. There won't be much of a security. Every club has a panic button. When it gets pressed, All the hitmen will arrive. It will take 15 minutes for the mob to reach the Irish club from the casino. unless Rudy keeps them busy. So remember you have to be quick."

Edward replies "Got it man, we will empty the club fast."

Bosco

" You loot the Irish club and bury the loot in the graveyard. Next day we will split the money."

Nathan
" Then what about the casino."
Bosco
" Casino was never the target. Its a suicide mission."
Nathan
" What if the Rudy comes up with the loot."
Bosco
" Then we will split it too but Rudy will never make it alive out of the casino. There is only one thing Michael should never know, Rudy is involved in this heist or he will never be a part of it, did you guys get it?"

Nathan and Edward replies, "Yeah we got it."

That night, Michael reached his place early. So it was the time for Michael to wish Veronica . Michael opens the terrace door and watches around there was no sign of her. Michael calls for her name in the dark twice, " Veron" and talks to himself, " I guess the birthday girl is sleeping." Michael turns back and opens the door to exit the terrace and she is in front of him.

Veronica
" How can i sleep without my birthday kiss."

Veronica hops on Michael and kisses.

Michael
" whow whow! easy Veron, you may break your gift."
Veronica
"Ohh my birthday gift. What is it?"

Michael removes a small pouch from his jacket. Veronica snatches it and starts unpacking the it, "Let me see what you got this year." She gets stunned after watching the gift. It was a chain, " wow! Such a beautiful chain." She kisses Michael and asks, " Is it gold."

Michael replies ," Of Course it's gold, look at the pendant it's a music sign. You love music don't you."

Veronica

" Ohh my sweet love, so thoughtful."

Veronica kisses Michael and they both start walking towards the edge of the terrace and get seated facing the view in front of them.

Michael

"Now tell, what happened at the performance?"

Veronica answered sadly,

"As usual, back in the chorus. I spoke with the organizer of the show. I begged him for a chance to sing and he said I don't decide who is gonna show up on stage. You will be there only if you have someone from the high table or big connections. One thing's for sure you need a godfather everywhere if you want to do something big."

Michael

" Nah ! You don't need anyone. Just be prepared sooner or later you are gonna get your chance. It's not your time yet."

Veronica snaps in anger, "Then when is my time?"

Michael requests her not to bring this up on her birthday night.

Veronica calms down and says, "Sorry" They take a pause for a few seconds and breath watching the view in front of them.

Veronica speaks, "Well how was you day."

Michael

" Like every other day, busting people and same old greedy Bosco, he is planning a new heist"

Veronica curiously, " Is it good."

Michael

" I don't know. I just told them i aint killing."

Veronica

"Yeah killing is bad, but how much money is involved."

Michael

" Can we talk about something else? Where is the cake?"

Veronica

" You are supposed to bring me the cake. There are pastries in your Mom's oven."

Michael

" How did you know this?"

Veronica

" Your Mom always makes it on my birthday. she knows I love them."

Michael

" She doesn't even know it's your birthday. "

Veronica

" You stupid horse, I saw her preparing for me from noon."

Michael

" Maybe it was for me, I told her to make pastries tonight. It has nothing to do with your birthday."

Veronica

" Now, you're getting on my nerves."

This continued the entire night, laughing, chatting, teasing each other. Michael didn't know when the sun rose that Bosco was gonna take the next step towards the heist. Which is gonna change everyone's life. It was the time when Bosco met a monster.

An injured girl dancing on a slow Chinese song in a house filled with wild men. Her face had a bruise. The guys in the house were throwing alcohol and cigarette buds. She is scared to death and she has been caught by the gang of Rudy. and she has to dance for them.

Bosco enters in front of the house and hears music outside the house. Bosco bangs on the door. A guy with the snake tattoo on the neck opens the door.

snake tattoo guy

" What do you want?"

Bosco

" I am here for Rudy ."

Tattoo guy starts closing the door saying, "There ain't no Rudy in here."

Bosco trying to explain, "Stop, I am suppose to be here."

Tattoo guy

" I know nothing man, just leave from here." Again he starts closing the door.

Bosco

" Stop, stop! I am leaving but listen to this. When I meet Rudy, I am gonna tell him that I came to your door and the deal went off because your boy didn't let me in. And I will also let him know this part, the guy who didn't let me in had a snake tattoo on his neck. I bet you that Rudy will kill you for the posy you're playing right now, " And he starts leaving from the door.

Tattoo guy stops Bosco and asks his name. Bosco tells him his name.

Tattoo guy shouts from the door," Rudy, hey Rudy "

Rudy looks at the tattoo guy. The guy informs Rudy that there's a guy at the door whose name is Bosco.

Rudy couldn't hear because of the music and he asks, " Who?"

Tattoo guy

" He says his name is Bosco. "

Rudy

" Who ?"

The tattoo guy shouts, "It's Bosco. "

Rudy hears Arnold and asks him again, "Arnold who? Who the fuck is he?"

The tattoo guy yells again, " Its Bosco , Bosco ."

Rudy gets annoyed and shoots the beatbox and the dancing girls scream in fear. Rudy asks again, " Tell me now who is it?"

" It's Bosco , he says he has a gig for you." Said the tattoo guy.

Now this time Rudy heard it clear and he said, " Yeah send him in, let him in. He is a piece of work."

The tattoo guy lets Bosco in. Bosco enters and watches the

environment," Looks like I crashed into a party. "

Rudy

" No the party's just started." and points the gun at the girl and says, "dance"

girl

" But there is no music."

Rudy

" Dance baby, I can hear an opera going on, " He closes his eyes and moves his head as if he is listening to music and starts humming." One guy throws cigarette on her," Dance you bitch move those titties."

Bosco

" Who's the girl?"

Rudy

" She and her guy were making love in the woods, " Pointing the gun at a dead guy lying in the room. " They always forget there are wild animals in the jungle."

Rudy screams, "Animals which are removed from society. Animals which are hungry."

Rudy asks Bosco, " Are you here for the girl?"

Bosco

" I got no business what you do to her."

Rudy

" Then what brings you here, " Takes a sip of alcohol from the bottle.

Bosco

"I have a proposition for you. A heist we will spit 50- 50."

Rudy

" What's the job?"

Bosco

" Bishops casino."

All the Rudy 's men start laughing and as Rudy looks at them everyone stops. Rudy moves his face at Bosco .

Bosco continues, "I got the map of the vault. I have the guns and the tools to break in and a exit plan too."

Rudy

" 60- 40, it's my men whose life will be on the line. I do the risky part. "

Bosco

" But without me you would never reach the vault."

Rudy

" Maybe i just kill you now, and take the map"

Bosco

" Do you really think I am that foolish to come here with the map and even if you did get the map? You don't have an escape plan. "

Rudy lights a cigarette and says, " 60 -40, take it or leave it."

Bosco

" Alright it's a deal. So we meet tomorrow at nineteen hundred in town hill graveyard and bring all the men you got. "

Rudy gives an evil gaze at him.

Bosco

" Come on, answer something? you are doing it or not?"

Rudy

" But why so soon? Why tomorrow? my men need time for preparation."

Bosco replies, " First I cant take the chance of someone tipping me off, that's the reason you know a day before. And second your men only need to shoot people and follow the map till the vault. which i see your men are good at." pointing at the dead body.

Bosco

" So my love i ask you one more time are you gonna do it or not?"

Rudy

" Alright i'll do it."

Bosco

" You will get every tool to set the casino on fire tomorrow night, see you at the graveyard." and he gets up and starts walking towards the door. Suddenly he stops, turns and says "one more thing, when this is over i want to know what you did with the girl" pointing at the girl, "I just love your work." and he leaves the house.

The tattoo guy from the door comes towards Rudy.

"Rudy , i think this is a trap."

Rudy

" Of course it's a trap. He agreed on 60 -40 because he is going to kill us after the loot." And he gets up and walks towards the girl.

Rudy

" Just make sure we have enough bullets even after robbing the casino" Removes his pants and grabs the girl's hair and drags her to the couch.

The tattoo guy

"That means we are doing it?"

Rudy

" Off course we are, just keep your finger on the trigger even there is no one to shoot."

The girl yells and screams in fear and Rudy starts raping the girl and the entire gang watches him rape in exitement.

The night of the heist. The reign of death and the plan of an evil man was about to take place.

Michael and Edward in a car. Edward is driving slowly and they both are checking out cars from their window.

Edward stops at a spot and says, " Look at that one." Pointing at a Chrysler across the street.

Michael asks, "The black one?"

Edward

"Yeah, its really fucking fast man. We need a fast car remember? "

Michael take's the metal rod and starts coming out of the car.
Edward warns, "Michael look around before you do it."
Michael listens and gets out of the car.
Edward from his car
"See you at the club Mike. " and drove away from there.
Michael hides the metal rod in his jacket while crossing the street. He comes near the car and looks around to see if there is anyone watching . Michael breaks the car window with a rod and opens the car from inside. Michael again looks around and gets in the car. He removes the wire behind the steering wheel and starts the car and driveS away from the sight.
As Michael enters Bosco 's card club, he watches people are playing as usual and there is no sign of his partners so he enters the private room and he watches Nathan , Edward check their guns.
Nathan gives a colt 45 to Michael, " Take this gun it's yours. Check it before you use it."
Nathan and Edward took a machine gun and a shotgun.
Michael
" Why I am getting the smaller one."
Edward
"Because you are gonna drive."
Michael looks at them in confusion and starts checking his gun.
Bosco enters the room
"Is everything ready? what about the car?"
Michael tugs the gun behind his back.
"I took care of that."
Bosco replies, "good. "
Bosco to everyone
" It will be a piece of cake but still watch out guys."
Croupier comes and informs them that the truck has arrived.
Bosco

" Yeah let him be but tell that motherfucker he is late, i will be right there."

Michael

" What's the truck for?"

Bosco

" I have to reach somewhere."

Michael

" You aint coming?"

Bosco

" No, I am the decoy."

Bosco yells at Michael

"For god sake Mike i will answer all your questions when you come back, for now just focus on the plan."

Bosco reminds the three of them again, " And remember to hit the place 15 min after the hitmen leaves the spot. Not a single minute before."

Bosco

" Best of luck guys we can do it." And they all hug each other and Bosco leaves the card club and gets in the truck and he starts driving. Michael, Edward and Nathan took the bag of clothes which they are gonna wear during the heist And also took the guns, a bottle of whiskey and got in the stolen car. Michael was driving and Nathan was next to him. Nathan loved the stolen car .

Nathan

" This is some fine piece of iron, can I keep it after the loot?"

Edward

"Don't you know what we are supposed to do at the end?"

Nathan

" Come on, this car is every guy's dream, I will paint it no one would recognize?"

Edward

" You will be painting your own death."

Bosco reached the graveyard; it was dark. The only lights were the headlamp of the truck. He could see only Rudy standing alone in the dark. Bosco stops the truck in front of him. Bosco gets pissed watching Rudy alone. He comes out of the truck and yells, "Are you out of your fuckin mind? We are looting a casino not a candy shop."

Rudy whistles and the men who were hiding in the graveyard came out with revolvers pointing at Bosco . They were 20 of them high on alcohol and drugs and were just ready to cause mayhem.

Rudy calms them down, "Its ok boys, he is the man who gonna make us rich."

Rudy to Bosco

" You are fuckin late."

Bosco

" Yeah I know, I was waiting for the guns to arrive. Come on check this stuff."

Bosco takes Rudy to the back of his truck , enters the truck container. There was no light inside. Bosco removes a small flashlight from his pocket and uses it to see the stuff he bought. He starts removing guns, bullet magazines, grenades and backpack from the toy boxes. Rudy gets overjoyed watching the machine guns.

Rudy

"Bosco you are a badass man this is some hardcore sheat. where did you get this ?" and starts checking the guns.

Bosco

" Don't ask."

Bosco removes the map and shows it to Rudy .

Bosco

" This is the map. We have to follow the red line drawn on the map. It will take us in front of an elevator then we get inside and go down it will take us to the vault. So make sure we go down to the basement."

Rudy

"And where is the key or the combination for the vault?"

Bosco walks towards a specific box.

" We have other options."

Bosco picks the box and starts unpacking it. Bosco shows him a time bomb? Rudy reacts, "Bosco, I think you are crazier than me."

Bosco

" You have to use the bomb for the vault."

Rudy

"It's a fuckin time bomb. I have only heard of them. I am watching it for the first time. I don't know how to use it."

Bosco picks the instruction sheet from the box and gives it to Rudy "Go throw the manual while we drive till the casino and memorize it."

Rudy comes closer to the time bomb, he watches there are two time bombs.

Rudy

" Why are there 2 of them? "

Bosco

" Incase we fuck up the first time." and he keeps the flash light there and starts walking outside the container.

Rudy

" Where the fuck are you going now?"

Bosco

"Don't i have to drive this truck. Get your sheat together, we will move from here in 5 minutes."

Bosco comes out of the truck and informs the Rudy 's men, "Gentlemen, go get your toys. We got a job to do."

Rudy 's men get inside the truck and start checking the stuff and start getting loaded.

Rudy to his men," Keep some extra ammunition with you. You guys know what to do when the time comes."

Michael, Nathan, Edward are waiting outside the Irish club in a car and they all have changed their clothes. Everyone is wearing black. Michael is sitting in the driving seat next to Nathan and Edward is in the back.

Nathan and Edward were singing the song "Row, row, row your boat song."

Michael

" How can you be so calm? We don't even know what are the horrors inside."

Nathan

" Don't worry, I know the place. Just wait until the hitmen leave. Bosco is working on it."

Michael

" What is the decoy?"

Nathan

" I don't know. He never shared a sheat."

Edward

" Even i asked, but he gave me nothing."

Rudy and Bosco are in the truck loaded with the weapons and men. Bosco is driving. Rudy is next to him and the men are in the truck container.

Rudy is going through the instructions, "First set the time then the red button."

Bosco

"Did you figure it out yet, how to use the bomb?"

Rudy

"Don't fuckin talk in between."

Bosco shuts up and watches the road.

Rudy notices Bosco has no gun on him

" Where the fuck is your gun."

Bosco

" I aint coming in."

Rudy

"Then where are your 3 monkeys?"

Bosco

" They are at the escape point. We can't stay here after this."

Rudy points the gun at him,

" I think you're setting me up."

Bosco

" If you want me to come, alright i'll come but i can't guarantee the escape."

Rudy

"This looks like a fuckin trap. I can smell it, you are up to something."

Bosco

"Look i brought the guns, bombs and the map to reach the vault. And this sheat is damm expensive, who will invest so much to trap you. and tell me nothing, what's between you and me? Don't doubt me. It's a loot, we have to run as far as we can and it's my job to look through it."

Rudy calms down and puts his gun down, " You better not fuck this up or your dead."

Bosco

"You think i don't know that."

Bosco continues driving and Rudy continues memorizing the bomb manual and starts touching the bomb.

Bosco gets a glimpse of him

"For god sake just don't set the bomb in the truck."

Outside the Irish club, Edward and Nathan are talking about chicks, drinking in the stolen car. Michael notices they hardly care about their lives and he is scared, worried and smoking cigarettes noticing the card club. He didn't care the number of cigarettes he smoked in that car, though there were a lot of his smoked cigarette buds outside his car. He also thought of his mother and Veronica , what will happen to them if he gets caught or dies?

Bosco heading towards the casino in speed and Rudy drinking and smoking next to him. Bosco puts his hand towards Rudy and Rudy gives him a smoke. Bosco smokes 2 drags and he watches from a 100 meters the casino's fancy flickering lights, "Alright we are here." and he throws the cigarette away and stops his truck right there by the street.

Rudy

"Why the fuck did you throw my smoke."

Bosco

" Seriously you wanna do this right now." and he takes a view of the casino.

The casino was ravishing and filled with crowds like every night. It was a happy environment. Everything was in its place but not for long.

Bosco starts his truck again and tells Rudy. "This will give you a little jerk."

Rudy says hold on a minute and he lights another cigarette and bangs behind him and says, "Boys, get a grip of something. " Then Rudy said to Bosco, " Come on do your thing."

Bosco pushes on the gas and the truck speeds up. In front of the casino a bald man stops his car, comes out, gives the car keys to the valet and walks to enter inside the casino . The valet was about to sit in the car and he notices a truck from behind speeding towards him and it's not gonna stop. He ran away from the car and the truck smashed the car.

Car owner was getting in and he turned back hearing the destructive sound and he was startled watching the accident.

The truck stops right there in front of the casino behind the wrecked car. Car owner watches that his car is badly damaged, "What the fuck just happened?" The crowd starts gathering near the accident.

The guards from outside inform every guard on the radio that there has been an accident outside. Few of the guards were coming out to check the accident.

Rudy 's men inside the truck container wear their masks and get ready with their guns and wait to pounce on Rudy 's order. The owner of the car was in agony and ran towards the truck driver seat, "You ugly little bastard, what have you done to my car."

Bosco screams from his truck, "Sorry! the brakes didn't work."

The car owner reaches at the Bosco 's side of truck," Come out you son bitch."

Bosco

" Hey man take it easy, it was not my mistake."

Rudy asks Bosco

" Now? "

Bosco watches at the entrance there were only few guards and he replies to Rudy," No, not now, let them gather."

Bosco continues answering the car owner and Rudy watches the guards at the entrance of the casino and smokes.

The car owner in rage, " come out you son of a bitch, you really got some heavy feet. I'll break them off for you. look what you done to my beauty."

Bosco takes a look at the wrecked car and says " i'm sorry i said it was the breaks"

Rudy signs Bosco by touching on Bosco's shoulder and Bosco watches in front of the casino there are very few guards. And answer nodding his head no. The guards from inside were still reaching towards the entrance to see what's the matter outside.

The car owner climbs on the truck from the side of the Bosco and grabs his neck , "I'll break your fucking neck, come out you bastard."

Rudy hides his machine gun under his seat from the car owner and he watches the casino entrance. Around 30 guards were gathered.

Rudy asks Bosco " now?"
Bosco watches number of the guards and replies, "yes now."
Rudy bangs behind at the container and says, "Its show time boys"
Rudy removes his gun from below the seat and the car owner notices and reacts, " ohh my god!" The car owner looks at Bosco's face, Bosco smiles at him. The car owner leaves Bosco's neck, gets down from the truck and runs away.
Rudy comes out of the truck and starts shooting at the guards with the machine gun. The guys from the truck also came out and started shooting. The crowd around the entrance of the casino starts running away. The gunshots sound panicked the crowd inside the casino and they all started screaming . The cashier inside the casino sets the alarm and few of the guards take the money to the vault.
The Irish club gets the information of the gun fight in the casino. The hitman informs his action team " Fellas the casino has been hit. we need to move." The hitman and his guys start picking their guns in hurry. The white haired guy from the card club asks the hitman while playing cards, "You want me to come?"
Hitman replies
" No you guys play. We"ll take care of it."
Hitman with his guys comes out of the card club and gets in their car and drives away to reach the casino. Michael and his team are watching them leave.
Nathan says " Whow! the countdown has just started, get your guns ready and keep counting the minutes."
At the casino, Rudy and his gang kill every guard outside the casino entrance and they throw grenades inside the casino before they enter. The grenade explodes then Rudy and his men enter inside firing with their machine guns. They shot everywhere and they made a mess of the casino.
The security guards from inside also fired back on the robbers. Rudy

's guys also got shot and 9 of them died on the spot. It was a massive gun fight. Rudy and his remaining gang reached the elevator following the map and they entered the lift. Rudy stops 5 of them from coming with him and tells them to wait on the floor and keep firing until he comes up with the money. Rudy and a few of his men enter the elevator.

In the basement, near the vault one guard was putting money in the vault and 3 of them were pointing guns at the lift. The guard moved all the money from the trolley to the vault and he turned after listening to the sound of the lift getting down. As the lift opens the guards shoot at the lift. Rudy uses one of his guys as a shield and starts shooting at the guards. The guards drop dead. Rudy comes out of the lift and watches one guard closing the vault. Rudy shoots him too.

One of Rudy's guys yells at Rudy, "Why did you shoot him, he might have the keys and the combination" and he walks towards the guard and watches him struggling to breath and a bunch of keys in his hand. The guy picks the keys and gets confused which one to use. Rudy starts searching a place to fix a bomb on the vault. Rudy to his men, " Key was never the plan and even i want to know how this sheat works."

Rudy's guys walk back and hide behind the wall. Rudy plants the bomb and starts setting the time. Rudy speaks to himself , "First set the time and then the red button." Rudy sets the bomb to 10 seconds and pressed the red button and he took the cover behind a wall. The bomb explodes and there was smoke everywhere. Rudy and his guys couldn't see a thing. Rudy watches the flames and he follows it. In a few seconds the smoke cleared and the vault was visible. The bomb opened the door of the vault and they saw it was filled with money. Rudy and his guys get stunned watching so much money. They remove the giant bags from their back and start filling them

with money.
On the road, the hitman in his car drove fast towards the casino. And outside the Irish club, Michael and his guys were breathing heavily, guns in their laps and were waiting for the 15 minutes to pass. Nathan watches time in his watch and informs " 5 minutes more."
Back at the casino heist, Rudy's men on the floor outside the elevator get shot by the guards. In the basement Rudy with his remaining guys fills their bags with money but there was still money left in the vault. Rudy throws a grenade in the vault and moves towards the lift his partners and replies, " i couldn't resist leaving so much behind." Rudy and his guys start getting inside the lift with loaded bags. Rudy orders his men to pick 2 of the dead guards. The lift alerts it is too heavy. one of Rudy 's guys says," It's too heavy, dump a body." Rudy throws the body out of the lift and shoots that guy in his head who suggested. The lift door closes, starts getting up and reaches the floor. As the elevator door opens the guards start shooting. Rudy and his guys were using dead bodies as shields. Rudy pulls the pins of the grenades and starts throwing outside the elevator. The grenade explodes, the guards get injured and Rudy and his guys come out of the elevator but still there are lots of guards. Rudy and his guys take cover and start shooting at them.
In the car, Michael, Nathan and Edward are watching the Irish club and waiting for the time to pass. As the minutes passed Nathan says, "Let go it's time."
Michael, Nathan and Edward put on their mask and Michael drives at speed and stops in front of the Irish club and they come out of their car with loaded guns. They enter the card club with a bang from the shotgun on the rooftop. After a few shots they stop.
Nathan
" Everyone, freeze, keep your palms on the table tops. We don't want to hurt anyone."

A croupier tries to press the alert button, Edward watches him and points a gun at him and says, " I wouldn't do that if i was you, put your hands up." The croupier puts his hand up and Edward hits his head with a shotgun.

Nathan knew that the bartender in the club had the key. Nathan catches him and asks him to open the vault. Edward and Michael stood there in the club pointing guns at the players watching their every Moment.

White haired guy to Edward

" Do you know who you're stealing from?"

Edward replies

" Just shut the fuck up you asshole."

One player tries to reach his gun from his pocket and Michael notices and he points a gun at him, " don't you even think of it." and takes his gun and throws it away.

Back to the casino Rudy and his guys are hiding behind the gaming machines.

One of the Rudy 's guy scream at Rudy, " It's impossible to get out of here, they are too many of them."

Rudy takes a bag of money sets the time bomb and puts at the bottom of the bag and covers the bomb from money and zips the bag.

The guy next to Rudy

" What the fuck are you doing? Why you want to blow the money?"

Rudy

"Just shut up and cover me."

Rudy 's guys start shooting to cover Rudy. And Rudy throws the bag of bomb near the guards. One of the guards checks the bag it's filled with money and he informs his shooting team, "It's the money. I think they want to surrender."

Every guard kept on shooting, they wanted to drop down Rudy and his gang.

The hitman from the card club reaches the casino with his action team, parks his car in front of the casino, comes out and enters inside the casino with their loaded guns.

Bosco smiles watching the hitmen entering the casino and speaks to himself, "bye bye Rudy " and breaks into a car parked away from the casino. There was no one to stop Bosco because no one cared at that moment. Everyone was running for their lives.

Inside the casino, Rudy loads his guns and tells his guys to wait for it.

The bomb from the bag explodes which was next to the guards.

Bosco was starting the car and suddenly he hears the sound of bomb and he stops and comes out of the car and watches casino entrance. He saw the hitmen who just went in and started coming out and there was smoke all over and then what he saw terrified him. It was Rudy with guns in smoke. Rudy and 4 of his guys came out with bags of money shooting at everyone.

Bosco watching him

"Son of a bitch made it out. "

Hitman watching Rudy says the same thing to his gang, "Fuck son of a bitch made it out, keep firing." The hitmen fired at them.

Rudy shooting and yelling outside the casino, "Bosco where the fuck are you? Where are you motherfucker? "

Rudy looks around and there is no sign of Bosco outside the casino.

Rudy continues shooting at hitmen and guards outside.

Rudy to his partner, "Bosco has fucked us, get in that car i'll cover you." points at the hitman's car. one guy sits in the front seat and throws the money bag in the back seat and shifts towards the driving seat and Rudy keeps shooting. Second guy also gets in the front seat and throws the money in the back seat. Third guy also gets in the car at the back seat and keeps the money down the seat. While they were entering the car Rudy was shooting at the hitmen.

Rudy asks the front seat guys to cover him, so he is getting in the car. The guys from the car kept on shooting at the hitmen.
Rudy gets in the car with the money. Rudy and 3 guys are in the car. He says," Son of a bitch Bosco framed me, start the car fast and take us out from here."

The guy from the driver's seat starts the car.

The hitman watching his car started checking his pocket, "Ohh sheat! the keys are still in the car."

There was one more guy left outside the car with his bag Rudy screams, "Come on get in"

The 4th guy keeps the bag in the car and was about to get in but he gets shot and he falls down next to Rudy's door. Rudy watches the guy dying and beg, "Rudy take me, please don't leave me."

Rudy to the dying guy

"Anyways there was less room in the car" and he shuts the door. Rudy breaks the back glass of the car and starts shooting at the hitmen and the driver of the car reverses and drives in speed towards the road, dogging the truck and the wrecked car. Hitman and his action team get in another car and follow them. Bosco gets scared watching Rudy alive and he knows Rudy will come after him.

Back to the Irish club, Nathan gets all the money from the vault in his bag. Edward is forcing the people from the table to put the table money, chains and rings in the bag. The white haired man denies giving his ring so Edward hits his head with the shotgun and snatches the rings from him.

Nathan warns Edward ," Hey fucker that's enough, we got to move now."

Now it was time to leave the club with the money. Michael, Nathan and Edward started walking backwards towards the exit door pointing their gun and warning everyone that no one moves. As they come out of the exit door they lock the door from outside and pull down the shutter and start running with the money towards the car. The counter guy presses the panic red button. Few guards from the club remove the hidden guns and rush towards the exit.

Nathan gives the money bag to Edward and tells Michael to start the car and he starts shooting the tires of the cars which were outside the club. Michael and Edward get in the car. Edward keeps the money in the back seat.

The people from the card club shoot at the door lock and open the door. Then they lift up the shutter and come out looking for robbers. Michael in the driving seat starts the car by rubbing wires and it's not getting started. Nathan enters the car and sits next to him.

Nathan screams, "Michael just start the fucking car."

Michael is trying his best to start the car. The guys from the Irish spotted the robbers car, "There they are."

Edward watches the Irish guys coming with guns towards them.

"Michael they are up to our ass, fuckin start the car."

The club guys start shooting at the car.

Edward and Nathan ducks down and yells

"Michael start the fucking car man."

One shot hits the back glass of the car. Fortunately the car starts and Michael drives away at speed from there.

The guys from the Irish club wanted to follow them but as they got near their cars they noticed the car tyres had been shot.

Rudy 's car is speeding on the street chased by the hitman and his guys. Rudy asks his guy to take risky turns. The guy behind the wheel is scared and panicked. Rudy tells," Just calm down, drive as if nothing happened. Remember if we make out of this mess alive, we are rich."

And Rudy turns back and shoots at the car chasing them.

Rudy's guy speeds up and takes risky turns and when he tries to overtake a car, his car gets hit by a truck coming from the front. The car was dashed real bad.

Hitman and his action team stop at a distance watching the crash.

Injured Rudy to the driver

"I told you to stay calm and drive."

Suddenly the blood splashes on Rudy's face. The guy next to him gets shot in the head. All the hitmen start shooting at them. The driver of the truck jumps out of the truck in fear. Everyone in the car gets shot. The hitman and his team were shooting non stop at the car. After a long shootout hitman stops his team from shooting. The smoke cleared and the car was in a mess.

The hitman

" Fuck man this are some serious holes."

Hitman watches there is no moment inside Rudy 's car and it had bullet holes all over it. Suddenly an injured guard from the casino enters the site and informs the hitman that there is a hit on the Irish club.

Hitman reacts, "what? what the fuck is happening tonight? Everyone just gets back in the car" and the action heads back towards the Irish club.

Michael, Nathan and Edward removes their mask and starts shouting and cheering in their car, "woohoo!"

Michael is also smiling while driving, Nathan is next to him and Edward is in the back with the money.

Nathan

"Check how much do we got?"

Edward

" I don't know maybe 10 or 20 lakhs or more, I can't tell and we have the jewellery too."

Nathan

" We got to pawn them."

Michael

" Not now, everyone will be looking for them. Relax for few days."

Michael, Nathan and Edward reach the graveyard and stop their car. They bury the money in the graveyard, change their car and clothes and head towards the club.

Michael, Nathan and Edward enter the club. People were playing like every other day, no one had a clue what happened outside.

Nathan asks Michael to stay at the bar counter as usual and asks Edward to get on a table and start playing. Next Nathan went into the private room. Nathan watches as Bosco was watching television and was shivering in fear. Nathan enters with a scream and Bosco gets scared.

Nathan in excitement, "Hey my man we fuckin did it." Nathan lifts Bosco up, "Come here darling give me a kiss."

Bosco in stress, "Just cut that out."

Nathan notices something is wrong with him, "what's with you now?"

Bosco

"Rudy made it alive."

Nathan

"what?"

Bosco

" Yeah."

Nathan

" If he is alive then we are fucked."

The news starts on television and they both start watching the t.v. The anchor talks about the heist at the casino and shows live footage and the casualties and Rudy got shot thrice after a long chase and he is in critical situation, the anchor also says Rudy is not gonna make it. After hearing this Bosco and Nathan look at each other and start cheering and laughing. Michael enters the room hearing their voice. Michael watches Bosco and Nathan making a drink.

Michael in low voice

"Keep it low. Your voice is coming outside."

Nathan

"Make this fucker a drink too."

Bosco makes a drink. Nathan comes closer to Michael, "Come here, have this." Bosco gives Michael a tequila shot.

Nathan

"Our plan worked, look over there." pointing at the television. Michael watches the news and says, " What the fuck? So this was your decoy."

Bosco

" It was his gig, he lost it. If Rudy would have been alive . We would have been dead. Look at the bright side. We are rich and never have to work again."

Michael watching the news

"That's lot of blood in our hands."

Bosco points at the television, "The people over there chose their fate. We had nothing to do with it. Rudy was gonna bust that place anyways. We just took the advantage of this situation"

Bosco to Nathan

" So how much do we got?"

Nathan

"I don't know? We didn't count. Shall we bring it here?"

Bosco

" You want to bring the loot money in front of all those people? let it be buried or it will be our grave. Now just act normal. We will complete our night and when everyone is gone we get the money and count at my place. We will be dead if we do a single mistake."

Suddenly the phone rings everyone looks at the phone in fear. Bosco walks towards the phone and answers it.

Bosco

" Hello! yeah, he is here" he turns and says, "Michael it's for you."

Michael heartbeat rises, "Who is it?"
Bosco replies, " I don't know."
Michael takes the phone in fear and he hears the voice of Veronica " Michael are you ok?"
Michael calms down hearing her voice," Yeah, I am fine."
Michael continues speaking on the phone with Veronica. Bosco and Nathan exit the room. Nathan asks Bosco who was on the phone? Bosco replies to some girl asking for Michael.
Veronica wiping," I got too scared. The news on the television freaked me out. I thought this was your heist."
Michael
" I told you I will never kill anyone. You know that."
Veronica
" Can you come her now i want to see you."
Michael
" I cannot come for a day or 2 you take care of mum."
Veronica
" Yeah Mike but you take care of yourself. Love you Mike."
Michael replies to her and keeps the phone and he heads out of the room and gets seated at the bar counter and watches Edward, Nathan and Bosco at the table.
One guy enters the club with the news of the heist.
guy
" Did you hear that? The casino and the card club got hit. robbers from the casino are dead but the club robbers are still at loose."
People from the club asked who it was.
The guy replies, "It was Rudy , who would do such a foolish thing rather than him. They all are gonna get caught. Its Bishop you know, he will find those rats."
Nathan , Edward and Bosco watch each other and hear the guy but they speak not a single word from their mouth. Michael drinking and

watching the conversation from the bar counter.
One more player enters, his friends ask him what took him so long? The player explains he had a long fight with the Cops. The Police stopped him and wanted to search his car. He denied so the fight started and later he came to know that there had been a hit at the casino. So without any more questions he let them search his car and he also said there's a lot of heat out there.
Suddenly another player shouts from a table
" Hey Bosco, you got any guns around here."
Everyone from the club stares at Bosco. And Bosco gets panicked after this question.
Bosco waits for a second and answers, "No, but why did you ask?"
Player
" The clubs are getting robbed, man. We are worried."
Bosco
" Don't worry, this is a small place. We don't make that kind of money."
Player starts playing again saying " Holly Christ, getting fucking paranoid because this sheat."
The night went as usual, players played the cards and left the club. Bosco and the gang waited till everyone made a move from there. And when the club got empty it was time to make their move.
Bosco
" Let's grab the money and get going."
Edward
" Didn't you hear what the guy said? Cops are all over the place. They are checking every inch whoever is out tonight."
Nathan
" Yeah man its a bad scene."
Bosco
" If the Cops or the Bishop men find the car used during the heist

they will search each and every coffin in that graveyard. We got to move the money. Or is there anyone who can move that car?"

Edward

"No man fuck no. Its too risky"

Bosco

" So we gotta take the risk."

Michael

"So why didn't you thought of this before."

Bosco gets agitated," I left this part ok. I had to do too much of everything. I didn't know every Cop would be out there searching for the robbers even after killing Rudy. If you want we can leave the money there."

Nathan

"Whoa! Calm down, no one is leaving the money. We will take it and move it at Bosco 's house."

So the gang decides to move the money from the graveyard. They all come out of the club and start walking towards their car. The gang was about to enter the car and suddenly a Cop puts a flashlight on them from their jeep.

Cop

" Stop! stay right there where you are."

The gang freezes and Cops come closer. The Cops start searching them for weapons. The Cops didn't find any.

Cop

" What the fuck are you doing here at this time?"

Bosco answers, " We were just heading home, this is our place" pointing at his club. "Just done for the night."

Cop

" Show me some id, and who are these guys?"

Bosco

" These are my partners."

Cop to his deputy

" Check their id and write down their names."

The deputy checks their id's and they also start searching the car.

Bosco

" Is everything ok officer."

Cop

" Yeah, some guys robbed Bishop's place. How stupid they are. They have called the death on themselves."

Michael and his gang watch each other in fear. The deputy informs the Cop that they found nothing in the car.

Cop

" Alright you are clean, You may go. I am sorry for the trouble Mr."

Bosco replies, " It's Bosco , my name is Bosco ."

Cop

" Yeah Mr. Bosco ."

Bosco

"No worries officer, you guys are doing a great job. I will be opening my casino soon. Maybe one day I might face the same problem. "

Cop

" Don't worry man, just get insured, that's all that you need. Alright good night casino man and drive safe."

The Cops leave from there in their jeep.

Nathan

" Casino man, what the fuck was about ?"

Bosco replies to Nathan

" Not now, when it's over."

Michael and the gang get in their car and head towards the graveyard. This time Bosco was behind the wheel. So now the plan is to dig the money back from the grave, put it in their car and keep it safe at Bosco 's house. The plan was a success but while reaching at the Bosco 's house they saw a Police check post on the street. Police were checking every car passing through the post. Bosco wanted to turn back but he couldn't. The Cops were also behind them. If they turn, the Police might suspect. So Bosco slows down his car. Nathan gets fed up and said, " Just out run them."

Bosco

" If we do that, we will be circulated on the radio and the entire Police force will be after us."

Nathan

" So what do we do?"

Bosco notices a 24 hours service restaurant by the road so he parks his car in front of the restaurant as if they stopped there to eat. Everyone gets out of the car and Edward starts opening the trunk

Bosco

"What the fuck are you doing? "

Edward

" Aren't we suppose to hide the money here?"

Bosco

" Are you out of your fuckin mind? Just get in the damm restaurant. If the Cops don't get anyone they will leave at dawn. just wait for it." Bosco and his guys get inside the restaurant. As they enter the waitress notifies," if your not buying the food and just gonna warm that couch drinking coffee so get the fuck out of here."

Nathan

" Alright what do you got?"

Bosco watches Nathan 's face

Nathan

" What! aren't we supposed to eat something?"

Waitress

" Here's the menu boys help yourself."

Nathan takes the menu card from the waitress and they settle down on a table. Nathan was checking on the list of food and Michael lit a cigarette and even Bosco took one.

Nathan

"I am gonna have a steak, and you Bosco ?"

Bosco

" Same as you."

Edward

" Is there Tacos in the menu card?"

Nathan

"No there are no Tacos here."

Edward

" Alright order steak to me as well."

Nathan

" You Mike. "

Michael

" No, nothing."

Michaels smokes his cigarette and looks outside the restaurant from the glass wall that the Cops are watching at the car. Bosco asks Michael for a lighter to light his cigarette and Michael points him out and Bosco watches one of the Cops coming inside the restaurant. Bosco signs this situation to his fellas.

Edward watching the Cop

" Oh sheat we are fucked."

Bosco

" Just shut the fuck up and speak nothing. Act as if you are supposed to be here."

The Cop asks the waitress who the car belongs to? The waitress points at the Michaels table. The Cop asks the gang in thick voice, "Is that your car?" pointing at the car outside.

Bosco

" Yeah it's mine."

Cop

" I need you step out, I want to search your car."

Bosco

" Look officer i have gone through this before, one Cop already checked us. "

Cop

" Do not argue otherwise you will face the consequences."

The gang comes out with the Cop. Bosco opens the car and the Cop starts searching.

The Cop while searching

" So what are doing here at this time."

Bosco

" I stopped by to eat something."

The Cop replies, "It's an awkward time to get hungry. it's almost dawn."

The Cop checked the car and now he wanted to check the trunk. The gang starts looking at each other's faces and they have no clue how to outrun the situation . The Cop tries to open the trunk but it's not getting opened.

Cop asked," How does it get? Opened" and he looks at Bosco and orders, " I said open the trunk."

Bosco

" You have to open it manually, The automobile is a junk."

The deputies behind them kept a hand on their gun.

Cop

" So give me the keys."

Bosco gives the keys to the Cop. The Cop inserts the key in the key hole of the trunk and it was about to get opened. Suddenly the previous Cop who checked Bosco and his car arrives, "Hey casino man." Everyone looks at the officer. The arriving officer informs the officer standing by the trunk that he has checked them before and these guys are clean.

The previous Cop to Bosco

" Why didn't you tell them?"

Bosco

" I did, they didn't listen."

The Cop stops from opening the trunk and gives the keys to Bosco and says, "You are good to go."

Bosco gets in the car with his fellas and the previous Cop comes at Bosco 's car window and says, "Hey casino man let me know if you got something for me. My name is Alex Tusk."

Bosco

" Sure, officer Tusk. i will let you know."

Suddenly everyone hears a sound of a woman screaming, "Robbers!"

Officer Alex Tusk turned back towards the sound and the gang from the car got scared.

Waitress from the restaurant complaining, " Officer catch those guys they food and now they are leaving without paying."

Officer Alex Tusk turns back to Bosco

" Now that's a crime. You got to pay for what you ordered for."

Bosco asks Nathan to pay the lady so Nathan comes out of the car and gives the lady money.

Alex Tusk

" I really like you man, i like the way you order people."

Bosco smiles and starts the car, Nathan gets back in the car and they head towards the check post.

Alex Tusk

"Good night casino man."

Cops stop their car at the check post. Bosco points at Alex Tusk.

Alex Tusk informs on the radio to the check post.

"Let them pass, they are clean."

The gang passes their car without getting checked at the post and they reach Bosco's place. Money, jewellery was on the table and all 4 of them were at Bosco's house. Bosco is counting the money in a counting machine.

Bosco

" Its upto 6 crores in cash."

Everyone cheers and Nathan throws the money up and shouts, "We are fuckin rich."

Edward

" I was tired of robbing people, card clubs and now we are free. We don't have to work anymore."

Bosco

" Who said so?"

Everyone stared at Bosco wondering what he was planning next. Michael made up his mind that if he plans another heist, he will not be a part of it. But Bosco's words were surprising. Bosco wanted to open a casino with the loot money and the entire gang agreed to him including Michael.

Now they have to build their own casino. It takes a lot of effort to make something so big . It includes the place, interior, gaming machines, gaming license and also wanted a stage for a singer. Officer Alex Tusk also helped the gang in many ways and for which he got paid. Edward even pawned the jewellery which he looted from the Irish club except a ring, he kept the ring for himself. It was tough but the gang made it possible. They named the club souls. Michael hired Veronica for the stage singer. In time the place started making serious money. Their investment paid them off. So parties, alcohol, expensive jewellery that was the game they know for now. Life was never better until the heist even for Michael. He is not a bouncer anymore, he is the head of security. The newly opened casino got too popular. Money was all around them. The place became famous all over Goa but remember this when you become rich then drugs always enter your life. In short, drugs are a rich man's game. Edward got addicted to sniffing cocaine and other chemicals.

As Veronica was hired as a singer in the club, she used to hangout with the gang. Michael, Veronica and the gang partied a lot together. Nathan had an evil eye on Veronica. He wanted to have her and many times he notices she is greedy for money but he didn't have an opportune Moment because of Michael being around. Until one night when George entered the casino.

George was in the casino playing cards. He lost all of his money but still he decided to play more and asked the card dealer to play on credit. The croupier denied. George started fighting with the card dealer.

George catches the card dealers collar and says

" Call on your boss, tell them it's me. They knows me who i am."

Michael was in the private cabinet eating food with Nathan , Veronica , Bosco and Edward. Edward is stoned and sleeps on the couch. The security informs Michael on a radio that there is a problem at the flash card counter.

Michael replies on the radio alright I'll be there. He just stops eating and runs towards the troubled spot and Michael sees George was fighting with the staff.

Michael calls on George

" George what happened?"

George

" This fuck wont buy me in."

Michael

" Alright buy him in, he is an old friend."

George to the card dealer

" Did you see this? What did he just say? come on now buy me in."

Croupier

"I am sorry sir, i didn't now"

George rubs his hand watching the game and talks to himself, "It's my time baby"

Nathan enters and shouts at the card dealer, " What the fuck do you think your doing? Why did you lend him credit? This old fucker will never return it."

Michael convincing Nathan , "Its George , he is a old friend"

Nathan

" So what, his wife didn't left any penny here."

George aggressively," You wanna talk about my wife, you street robber."

Nathan replies, "Why don't you ask her who I am."

George

" I know very well who you are and where the money came from. You think I won't come to know what you guys have done. My silence is keeping you alive boy."

Bosco enters between the fight, "Come on George, what's going on?"

George

" Ask your boy?"

Bosco calms George, " You know he is a nutcase. George this is your place, come in anytime you like. Now stop playing and we are having dinner together."

Bosco orders the card dealer to give back George's money which he has lost in the game and Bosco takes George into his private cabin.

Michael, Bosco , Edward and Veronica are in the cabin with George eating, drinking and talking about old times when they were together.

Veronica looks at the time and speaks with Michael, "Hey Mike it about time, i got to get on stage." She kisses Michael and leaves the cabin.

George speaks to Michael about Veronica after she exits," That's a pretty girl you have Mike. Get married now, stop fooling around."

Michael

" Yeah, we are planning."

George
" Stop planning and just get it done, marriage at the right time is very important."
Nathan enters the cabin and George stops speaking and leers at him. Nathan gives back the game money to George which he lost at the counter. George is still watching Nathan in anger.
Nathan
" Come on now George, I am sorry for what is said, it will never happen again." and he sits next to Edward and wakes him saying, "Wake up you bitch."
Edward is stoned and replies." Let me sleep man, my head is spinning."
Bosco to George
" Why were you even playing here and losing? This is your club you are the new security incharge over here."
George
" Thanks guys. but I am happy where i am."
Nathan opens the Champagne and fills the glass," We know you wont work for us but still we love you and you are our friend and will always be." raises his glass, "To George."
Bosco and Michael also raises their glass," to George." and they all drink. As Nathan kept his glass on the table, he picked the Champagne bottle and said, "George, I think it's your time."
George
"What?"
Suddenly Bosco holds the hands of George which were lying on the table and Nathan starts beating George's head with the thick bottle until he bleeds. It was too late for Michael to stop; he was shocked by what he just saw. George bleeds from his head and gets unconscious.
Edward wakes up with his eyes wide open
" What the fuck man ?"

Michael

" What the fuck have you done Nathan ?"

Nathan

" He was danger to all of us."

Bosco

" He could have fucked us one day. He knew we were behind the loot."

Michael

" So you killed him?"

Nathan

" So what do you suggest? Talk him out of this and make him our partner."

Bosco

" We cannot take risks. All of this will be gone for good."

Edward speaks in a very slow voice, " There is lots of blood on the floor man."

The guard informs Michael that the Police are on its way.

Michael to Nathan and Bosco, "The Police is here."

Bosco

"Relax, I got a meeting with Officer Tusk. Mike gets rid of the body, burying this sheat. Nathan, did you keep the burying tools in the car?

Nathan

" Yeah it's done."

Bosco orders Nathan , "So now you better clean this mess up. " pointing at the blood on the table and floor.

Edward asks," what do i do?"

Nathan

" You better get up and help Mike."

Edward

" I ain't touching that body."

Nathan in rage," Get your ass up, you junkie." and he kicks Edward in the chest and Michael is stupefied watching all this.

Bosco

" Hurry, we don't have time. Veronica will be here any Moment. Take him from the back side, I have parked my car there." and he throws the keys at Michael and leaves. Michael in confusion watches Bosco leave and then he looks at the dead George.

Veronica was singing, ' Diamonds are forever' song on the stage and the crowd was enjoying her voice and at the same moment Michael, Nathan and Edward put George in a plastic bag. Michael and Edward lift the body and start taking out of the cabin and Nathan throws the bottle in the trash can and picks the mob to clean the blood. Bosco met officer Alex Tusk at the playing zone and watched Veronica on stage. Michael and Edward take the body out of the casino from the back door. Edward hears the song and asks, "Is this is your girl singing?"

Michael

" Yeah."

Edward

" Maybe i'll listen her song then i'll come back and help you."

Michael

"Have you lost it completely?"

Edward

" I was just kidding."

Michael and Edward put George's body in the trunk of Bosco's car. Then Michael gets in the car with Edward and heads towards the graveyard and at the same time Nathan is cleaning the blood stains from the cabin floor.

Michael drives and watches a Police check post on the street. Edward gets panicked. Michael tells him to calm down and don't speak. The Cops recognize Bosco's car and they let them pass.

Back in the casino, the audience claps after the Veronica's

performance and she leaves the stage and enters in the cabin calling for Michael, " Mike did you saw my performance."
Nathan was alone in the cabin smoking and watching officer Alex and Bosco sitting in the playing zone from the glass widow.
Nathan answer Veronica, "Michael just left, he had to take care of George ." And continued watching Bosco and Alex
Veronica
" Fuck i need a hit."
Veronica sits on a couch and snorts coke from the table. Nathan watches officer Alex Tusk leave and then he sits next to her.
Veronica, "How am i gonna get to my house Tonight.?"
Nathan
" Don't worry, i'll drop you."
Veronica
" Mike is very irresponsible; he never cares about me. What I feel like, what I want. He is just too dumb to understand."
Nathan
"Well you made a wrong choice. What are you even doing with a guy like Mike, he is just a security guy. You are the star of this casino, you don't deserve a guy like Mike. Find a King who will treat you like a Queen."
Nathan removes his ring from the pinky and puts in Veronica's ring finger.
Veronica keeps watching the red stone on the ring.
Nathan
" Don't worry, its ruby."
After listening to his words Veronica starts kissing Nathan desperately and Nathan lifts her and makes her sit on his lap and Veronica starts removing her clothes.
At the same time, Michael reaches the dark graveyard, he stops his car and looks at Edward. Edward says that please don't make him do

this. Michael understands what he was going through. Michael comes out of the car and removes the body of George's by himself. He also picks the flashlight, shovel and mattock from the trunk. Michael takes the body to a spot and starts digging with his tools.

Back in the casino, Nathan is making love to Veronica on the couch and Bosco enters the cabin and gets shocked watching them together. He notices that the couch on which she was lying was covered with money and this view explains Bosco a lot about the situation. So he starts removing money from his secret vault. When Nathan is done Bosco also fucks her on the same couch and puts money all over her body. After that Nathan picks Veronica up and makes her stand. She puts her arm around his neck and lifts her one leg up and tugs on Nathan's back and Bosco holds her from behind and helps her lift the other leg. Veronica gets double penetrated.

Back in the graveyard, Michael has dug a hole in the graveyard and Edward is sniffing cocaine in the car. Michael comes out of the hole and lifts George and puts him in and starts putting mud with the shovel. Michael notices George is moving. He comes down, tears the plastic from George's face and finds George is alive. George was suffocated and he tried to breathe for seconds and then he begs, " Mike don't bury me alive please let me go, what have I ever done to you."

Michael

" I am sorry George, i have to do this."

George

" Give me a chance Mike, I will take my wife and leave Goa for ever. You will never see me again."

Michael

" You have nowhere to go, your wife is also involved. If I leave you alive then my death is for sure. You have to die George ."

George

" Don't do this Mike, don't do this. I beg in front of you. Let me live please. We have been friends for so long."

In the casino cabin Veronica, Bosco and Nathan are sitting nude on the couch. She lights up a cigarette and asks both of them," What happens when Mike finds out?"

Nathan

" He will never, don't you worry we know how to fix him."

Nathan and Bosco look at each other and start smiling. They got an evil plan to frame Michael.

Next day, Michael was sleeping in his house. He has bad dreams of George getting buried and George speaks while getting mud on his face, " Mark my words they will bury you too." and his mother wakes him up. Michael wakes up in sweat. Michael asks his mother what happened and why did you wake me.

Mother.

"Michael, there is one lady with the Police officer at our door. Did you do something last night?"

Michael gets up and he comes out of his room. Michael watches as George's wife is with officer Alex Tusk. As she watches Mike she starts yelling and screaming, "You bastard what have you done to my husband. Officer that's the guy, he is the one" pointing at Michael.

Michael

"What are you talking about?"

George's wife

" Ask him, officer? What has he done to him?"

Michael's Mom is scared to death and worries that Michael did something wrong. Michael had no words, he didn't even know what to answer. George's wife kept on accusing him.

Officer Alex asks the deputy to shut her up. The deputy stops her from talking and then Alex starts asking questions to Michael.

Officer Alex

" I got a complaint against you Mike. Where were you last night?"

Michael

" I was at the casino. why?"

Officer Alex

"I know last night George went crazy. Things went a little rough between you and George and from last night he went missing. No one has a clue where he disappeared."

Michael

"Things were never bad between me and George. I just stopped the fight and that's part of my job."

George's wife

" Then who was it, Nathan? He would never do such a thing. You bastard are the one who had done something to him," and starts crying loudly. "Ohh my poor George , where are you?"

Officer Alex to deputy.

" Officer will you take her out!"

The deputy takes the crying George's wife out of the house and Alex speaks with Michael alone.

" Look Mike I know you but his wife complained about you. You know how it works. It's a Police formality. I have to take you to the Police station for your statement." Comes closer to Michael, "Don't worry i got your back." And he walks out of the house.

Michael start wearing his shirt and Mom asks distressingly, "What's going on Mike ?"

Michael replies, "It's nothing Mom, i'll be back in sometime."

Mom questions again," Then what is this all about? have you done something wrong?"

Michael

" No Mom, I did nothing wrong." and he gets out of the house and his Mom watches him go with the Police and she didn't know it was the last time she was watching Michael.

While sunset Michael entered the casino worried. Veronica was singing a 'rapture' song on the stage. Michael walks towards the table where his gang was settled watching Veronica's performance. Michael reaches the table and speaks to Bosco anxiously, "Bosco, the heat is on me. There was a Cop at my house today . I was 2 hours in the Police station for 2 hours. The Cop took my statement but i gave them nothing."

Bosco asks," Which Cop that one over there." points at officer Alex sitting in the crowd.

Bosco

" Just relax , I got it all covered up. George's wife filed a complaint against you. There are few witnesses you both had a fight."

Michael lights a cigarette," But this is insane. I didn't do anything."

Bosco, "I know. But she will never go against Nathan."

Veronica watches Michael talking to the gang and even Michael looks at Veronica singing, she smiles looking at him.

Bosco

" All you have to do is disappear for few months."

Nathan

" Yeah man i will calm her down in some time, but you shouldn't be here."

Michael, " Is there any other option."

Bosco

" If you wont go, the Cops will keep on coming here and the club will be pulled in the investigation. There will be a lot of noise about you and this place. Then there are chances, we all might get caught and this place, everything will just shut down. All our hard work will burn into ashes. Do you want that?"

Michael watches at Veronica singing."fuck what have i got myself into?"

Edward is stoned again," Mike relax, you go to Mumbai . I have my cousin there. He is a wild hog. He will take you in and teach you a lot of new things. Everything is sorted."

Nathan

" Don't worry, we will call you as it gets over."

Veronica's performance gets over and everyone claps, even the gang. She leaves the stage and while going she smiles looking at Michael. After a few drinks with his gang in the casino, Michael speaks with Veronica in the cabin on the couch and the entire gang is watching their conversation.

Michael

" Veron, tonight I'll be leaving for Mumbai. Are you coming with me?"

Veronica

"But why ?"

Michael looks at the gang for a second and answers her," I can't tell you the reason. Tell me do you wanna come with me?"

Veronica

" I can't, I got a good thing going here and even your Mom is alone. Who will take care of her? Have you thought about that? You just keep on making plans why are you even leaving Goa."

Michael

" I have to Veron, i can only say it's for the betterment of everyone's future."

Veronica

" I would have come with you, but I cannot leave your Mom at this age. You know old she is."

Michael looks away thinking of Mom

" Yeah my Mom. Listen, tell her I had to go out for business and take good care of her. i'll be back in few months."

Veronica starts crying

" ohh Mike, why do you have to do this ? What will i do without you ?"

Edward speaks comforting Veronica , " Don't you worry. He is in safe hands. Actually he is lucky people die to live in Mumbai ." Then he tells Michael, " Come on Mike it's time."

Michael is sad that he has to leave Goa, speaks in a very soft voice, " Take care of yourself, Veron. Don't forget I love you. " Michael hugs her and he kisses her goodbye then he gets up from the couch and walks towards Bosco. Bosco gives him a small bag of money," Here's some money. if you need anything. You just have to give a call."

Nathan

" Don't worry man, we will call you as things get sorted here."

Michael and Edward leave the cabin and Veronica is still crying on the couch looking down, covering her face with hands. Nathan and Bosco watch her cry.

Nathan

" Stop it now, he is gone."

Veronica looks up at Nathan and Bosco and her eyeliner is all over her face because of her tears, "Are you sure?"

Bosco

"I am damn sure."

Veronica removes the ring from her bra which Nathan gave her and wears it.

"This bitch is an evil man." Nathan whispers to Bosco .

Veronica starts making a drink for herself on the table placed in front of her, "Thank god he left, i thought he would never go." Gulps the drink and lights a cigarette and watches her face in the purse mirror, "This crying act spoiled all my fucking make up." Starts wiping her face with a cloth.

Nathan

" What an actress? You are really good at this Do you know that?"

Veronica

" Practice makes you perfect. I have been doing this for years. He

thinks I am gonna throw away all of this for his love. Foolish chap."
Nathan and Bosco sit next to her on the couch and they start removing their shirts.

Nathan

" Don't throw me away from you my love."

Veronica

" Never, this will never happen."

Veronica kisses Nathan and then Bosco. And their threesome starts again.

Poor Mike, getting played by everyone. At least Edward is with him but not for long. Michael is headed to the airport in Bosco's car driven by a driver. Michael and Edward are in the back seat and they both are depressed.

Edward

" Don't you get sad boy, I got your back. I will take care of your mama and Veron, don't you worry. You just enjoy your time there. My cousin will pick you up from the airport. His name is Peter. You will be fine there." and he snorts cocaine in the car.

Michael

" You get a grip on this stuff. It might cause you serious damage."
Edward replies," Yeah only if i try to live sober." They both start laughing.

Edward

" Don't worry about me man, nothings gonna happen to me. Here's something for you." Edward removes the ring from his finger and gives it to Michael, "Take it, it's for good luck."

Michael

" The good luck we stole."

Michael denies taking the gold ring, " Nah, you keep it, looks good on you." Then Edward starts removing his gold chain from his neck.
Michael gets annoyed, " I don't want the chain either."

Edward

" It's not for you, it's for Peter. You give him when you reach there."

Michael wears the chain and the driver stops the car.

Edward yells at the driver, " Why the fuck did you stop?"

Driver replies," Sir we have reached."

Edward

" I wish we had more time man."

Michael

" It's ok, it's time to say goodbye, I hope the time I will spend in Mumbai will be shorter."

Edward

" And I wish that from now the time flows faster."

Michael

" Then what is the fun in living? See you later Eddy . take care."

Michael takes his bag of money and steps out of the car. He starts walking towards the airport. Edward also comes out of the car.

Edward

" Mike wait."

Michael stops and Edward comes closer to him and hugs him and says, " I am gonna miss you man. I am really gonna miss you." Stops hugging, " My huge man Mike. Teach me how to box people when you come back. Do you Remember how tiny you were when i first saw you?"

Michael

" Yeah You were the one who caught me in the factory."

Edward looks down in guilt, "I feel life would have been different for you if you didn't show up in the factory that day." Michael says, "And you were the only one waiting outside the window till I came out."

Edward gets emotional and tears in his eyes

" I am sorry Mike, sorry for everything."

Michael replies, " Yeah me too"

Edward wipes his tears
" Come on now, enough of this sissy talk, just go and take care of yourself. its only for few days."
Michael replies," I really hope so. Good bye Eddy ." and he turns and walks towards the airport and Edward watches him go till he enters inside the airport and then he gets back in the car and reaches the casino and gets shocked after watching Veronica drinking and partying with Bosco and Nathan .
After a few hours, Michael reached Mumbai . It was the first time when Michael stepped out of Goa. Michael was heading out of the airport and there he saw a guy with a sign board and his name written on it. Michael walks towards him and they meet . It was Peter. As Peter confirms it's Michael his first words were "Lets go, i have no time. I got a place to run." Peter walks out and Michael follows him. They get in a car. The guy who was driving the car was freakishly huge, thick black colored, curly hair and gold chains in his neck. By looking at him Michael realizes he ain't no driver and whatever Peter is doing is not legitimate. Michael prepared himself for what's coming next.
Peter in his car asks Michael, "So how is my cousin?"
Michael
" He is high on drugs."
Peter
" He is always high on something."
Peter watches the chain at Michaels neck.
Peter
" Nice piece of shine on your neck."
Michael
"ohh it's yours. Eddy gave me to hand it to you."
Michael removes the chain and gives it to Peter and Peter wears it.
Peter

" Same old Eddy always gifting everyone because he got a gift too."

Michael

"What is it ? "

Peter

" Being alive."

Michael looks at Peter with his eyes wide open.

Peter

" Yeah, he stole my mothers jewellery and ran to Goa. That's how he met you guy's. For years I was searching to kill him."

Michael

"Then why are you helping his friend?"

Peter

" Well he is family, we all have to forget family grudges and beside that i heard that you are a piece of work"

The driver stops the car in the slums of Dharavi, the biggest slum in Asia and they both get out. Then Peter starts getting into the slums and Michael follows him. Michael didn't ask where he was taking him, he just walked behind Peter into the slums. The place was smelly, small lanes, houses attached to houses, thick black gutters and twisty, zigzagged ways like a maze. Peter looks back and watches Michael is still following and Peter smiles.

Peter

" We have to keep a low profile. We cannot be out in the open. If Police wants to catch us it will take an entire day to find us, by the time we fly."

Michael got confirmed that Peter is into illegal activities but he didn't know yet what Peter is into and finally they reach their spot. There were black huge guys with weapons in a tiny lane outside a house. A man could die in fear even if these guys stare at them. And now I have to live with them. Peter enters a house and Michael follows him. There were ugly looking people playing cards, Peter again looks back and speaks to Michael, "This is just the front waiting for some real fun" Peter walks further passing the card club and enters a door with Michael . Michael watches it was a brothel and there were 10 by 10 feet boxes and every box there was a woman. The only thing which covers the box was curtains and those women were getting fucked inside. The place was smelly. Michael was disgusted watching the place. Peter asks, "Tell me if you want some one for the night?" Michael didn't bother to answer him. Peter didn't just stop there, then he entered one more door passing the boxes and Michael followed. That was the last room of the slum castle. Michael saw the place was filled with drugs and machine guns. The guns were just lying on the floor as if they were toys. Michael got an idea what Peter was doing. He runs a card club, brothel and smuggles. After the Irish heist he decided that he will never choose a wrong way but he was away from his house, casino and the money which he had wont last for a month. He had no options. Peter tells him to rest here for now and he will fix him at a nice place the next day. "

Michael couldn't sleep so he started drinking and watching the place around. He saw the hookers getting fucked, people playing card games, peddlers buying stock of drugs and even young children coming there for small amount of dope. Michael noticed Place was disgusting but it was making more money than the casino and he drank till he passed out and he saw his mother in his dream. That mother is seated in a wooden chair in a dark room calling, "Mike where are you? Something is wrong Mike? Come home quickly?" and suddenly blood starts coming from her head and all over on her face. Mom starts wiping the blood from her face and as she puts her hand down the face changes into Veronica and she speaks, "How's the start Mike? this is just beginning of becoming a boss." her voice gets thicker, "Or the end of your life." Michael wakes up in fear and he finds himself in one of the boxes and he comes out of it. Michael looks around and everyone is asleep. Michael watches Peter sleeping naked with 2 prostitutes and their hand and legs were wrapped around him. Michael checks the time it was noon and walks towards the nearest window and opens it and the sunlight wakes Peter. Michael noticed Peter opened his eyes. Peter tells, "This is Mumbai our morning is at the sunset, go back to sleep and close the window." Michael closes the window and Peter his eyes. Michael passed the day by checking the guns in a room but he didn't go out because he knew he would get lost, out in that maze.

When Peter wakes up he takes Michael to a flat with a sea view on the top floor of a building. Michael keeps on watching the view. Peter asks, "Did you like the place?"

Michael replies, "Yeah."

Peter

"You can stay here if you like but I have to live at Dharavi to run that place."

Michael keeps watching the sea and Peter asks, " Did you like the view?"

Michael replies, " It's a beauty."

Peter

"You know why I like this view?"

Michael

"Why?"

Peter

"By looking at the sea I realize we can always get our hands dirty because there is plenty of water. We can always wash them off."

Michael turns his face towards him. Peter asks one more question which messes with Michaels head, "Well how were the machine guns and the bombs?"

Michael

"What are you talking about."

Peter answers, "Ohh i forgot, if you would have been in the action you would have been dead too." Peter leaves from there and Michael keeps on thinking, watching the sea for hours figuring that it was Bosco who framed Rudy and made the Bishop's casino a slaughter house so he could rob the Irish club.

Peter starts taking Michael to his meetings. Michael met big gangsters of Mumbai and also participated in Peter's dirty work, dealing drugs, smuggling in docks, emptying weapon cargo from the ship, and running Peter's place in Dharavi. Michael learned the work too quickly. He also handled the local buyers. The gang from Dharavi liked Michael being around. Michael was involved in the business completely. Peter believed in him, he really was a piece of work. So he shared a problem with Michael while he was playing carom in Dharavi with his gang.

Peter

"Michael there is a problem."

Michael

"What is it?"

Peter

" We have the Police and the politicians but a reporter is always grabbing us in action. He wants to just expose us, our water transport is in trouble because of him."

Michael

"Do you know where he lives?"

Peter

" I don't even know his name and what he looks like."

Michael, " So let's find out." Michael and Peter play a posy. Michael sends Peter many times on docks at night for no reason. The game was that Peter only had to be there talking with the people he didn't even know and Michael would stay hidden for the reporter to show up and take pictures. And it worked. One day hidden Michael saw a guy taking a picture of Peter and he followed him till his house. Now Michael knows where he lives. So Michael wears a mask and breaks into the reporter's house and cripples him, burns all the pictures he took and puts the reporter in a cargo of a ship which was headed to a middle east country.

In Goa, Bosco and the team keep on making money and Veronica is always with them. They are always partying in restaurants and clubs. Edward is always stoned. One night Michael calls on the telephone of the casino and Nathan answers his call. Michael asks, " When can I come back?" Nathan replies, "Still there is lot of heat Mike you cannot come here."

Michael

" Where is Veron? I haven't spoken to her. "

Veronica was right there next to Nathan biting his ears but he lied, " she is not here, she spends most of her time taking care of your mother."

Michael gets relaxed after listening that his Mom is not alone Veronica is with her.

Michael continues working with Peter and deals with the guns too. Michael came to know that the machine guns which were imported to India were from China and exported to the local buyers like Naxalites, Local gangsters and robbers. When he met the Chinese dealers they shared a secret with Michael, that China has an art of technology and they have spies in every industry and every field to grasp the knowledge of a product. Michael even smuggled gold from Dubai to India and he also did business with various foreign country dealers for guns and drugs and it was highly profitable. Michael had the courage to act, talent to perform and will to get the job done.

Back in Goa, Nathan, Bosco and Edward visit Veronica's house at night. Michael's Mom hears loud music, and laughs from her house and Mother realizes that Veronica doesn't care about Michael, she just used him all his life to get what she wanted. Bosco and Nathan were drinking, snorting and fucking Veronica together in front of Edward.

Edward watching them," It's wrong, it's so damn wrong. You cannot do this, Michael is our friend."

Bosco replies," Michael is long gone. And are we raping her? she has no problem doing this then what's yours? "

Nathan

" Join us or leave us, the choice is yours."

Edward takes the whiskey bottle and gets out of the room and he notices Michael's Mom at her door and while passing through her he says, " I always knew this world is not a good place but there is somewhere goodness inside everyone. The people back there." pointing at Veronica 's house, " They are rotten, they don't have any soul." Edward takes a sip of the whiskey and leaves from there. After that night Bosco and Nathan often visited Veronica's house and Michael's Mom noticed them several times. The stoned Edward never came back there because he couldn't watch the dreadful act of his partners and the most important part he just couldn't face Michael's Mom again. He knew his partners tore Michael's world apart.

Back in Mumbai, Michael got more deeper into the game. Though the business was dirty, he was honest to everyone. The entire Dharavi gang respected him. He continued smuggling of guns, drugs and gold. In this crooked business there are crooked people. Michael spoke when he had to, used his brain when he was supposed to and he used his hands and weapons when he needed to. Michael also partied with the gangsters of Mumbai , he was a known face to everyone but every night he thought of his mother and Veronica. The money which he made was larger than Peter used to make, he gained so much because of his moral nature towards the gang. He had everything but his heart was in Goa. He called up every night at the casino but the gang always used to avoid talking to him and hung up his call. The gang was drowned in lust, greed and drugs.

In Mumbai, the business got bigger and more men were involved and they needed more space for goods and money. Michael took a decision to free the woman from the whore house without Peter's concern. And that night Peter got mad at Michael.

Peter in rage

" What do you think of yourself? How can you just free the girls? those were my goods."

Michael replies, " We need space to keep some stuff."

Peter asks, " What stuff?"

Michael removes the curtains from the boxes where women used to live. The entire boxes were filled with drugs and weapons. Peter gets stunned watching it.

Peter

"Do you have any idea how much time it's gonna take to sell this stuff?"

Michael

" You don't have to, I am buying in cheap and selling at 10 times more to our buyers. The rate is still less for them than usual. The local buyers also decided to buy in big quantities. "

Peter

" Do you know how risky is this?"

Michael

" I know more the money, more the risk."

Michael supplied the stock to his buyers in an ambulance, dead coffins, and inside fish and meat. And the Dharavi brothel has become a warehouse filled with goods. The guns were also shipped to other countries. Michael went international and slowly the entire Peter's brothel was filled with money.

One night, George 's wife watches Nathan passing in a car. She screams for him, Nathan didn't listen and she got a 2 second glimpse that Veronica was kissing him. The car just went away. She just rushed home, drank in agony and broke every mirror in anger. George 's wife was anguished. She did everything Nathan said and when he was done using her, he didn't even care to meet her. She was heartbroken but was not in love. Her motive was only sex and glam life which Veronica was living.

One night, Michael calls at the casino and Veronica picks up the phone while she was snorting with the gang.

Veronica answers, "Who the fuck is it?"

Michael

" What the fuck is happening there? "

After hearing Michael's voice Veronica gets a shock and stops the gang from speaking.

Veronica

" Nothing Mike, tell me how are you?"

Michael

" I am fine. Why are you not answering my calls?"

Veronica

" How would I Mike? When you left for Mumbai I hardly came to the club. I am always at home."

Michael

" I have done enough time here. I'll be there soon.

Veronica

" But the George case."

Michael

" So you know what happened?"

Veronica

" Yeah Mike, I have ears. I heard you killed George "

Michael

"This is bullshit, I didn't do anything. I will tell you when I get there. i'll

be there soon"
Veronica
" But the case is still going on"
Michael
" Fuck the case, i have contacts now and some money too, i can handle this sheat now."
Suddenly George 's wife bangs the door and enters the cabin in rage, "Where is that bitch?"
Everyone in the cabin just got startled watching George 's wife.
Michael on the phone," Who is that ? What's going on there?"
Veronica replies," Mike it's nothing i'll call you back." and she hangs up.
George 's wife watches Veronica on the couch keeping the phone, "There she is."
George 's wife runs towards Veronica in aggression and pounces on her. She grabs Veronica 's hair and scratches her face, " You are taking my man away from me you bitch. I am gonna kill you."
Nathan enters their fight and grabs George 's wife and takes her away from Veronica but she is still struggling to catch her back.
Veronica is petrified.
Nathan speaks " whow whow! easy girl. stop it."
George 's wife
" Get your hands off me. I did everything for you, betrayed my husband, helped you in the heist, even framed Michael because of you. And you left me for this bitch."
Edward screams from the couch after hearing about the betrayal " What the fuck have you done Nathan?"
Nathan turns back and replies," Not now Eddy ."
George 's wife
" You just took advantage of me, used me to reach here and now when you are done, you just throw me away." and starts crying.
Nathan holds George's wife in his arms, " It's only you, no one else.

You are my only girl. You know I love you. Just calm down.
George's wife gets away from Nathan and wails," Liar."
Nathan, "Look this is not the right time or a right place. We need to talk in private, i'll come by the house tonight and we will talk. Come I'll walk you till your car. Just relax baby i love you." and he puts his arm around her shoulder and takes her out of the cabin.
Veronica's hair was all messed up and she had scratches on her face," Fuckin bitch, ruined my face."
Veronica asks Edward," Are the scratches on my face deep?"
Edward replies," You deserve worst than this."
Veronica, "Die in hell you junkie."
Bosco
"Fix your hair. You got to get on stage. You look like a mess."
Veronica replies, " You guys are in a mess too. Michael is coming."
Bosco in shock
" ohh sheat !"
Edward laughs
" hahahahah, you guys are in a sheat, lot of deep sheat."
Nathan enters and watches. Edward laughing,"What did i miss?"
Bosco informs Michael is coming.
Nathan gets shocked too,
"No, no, no, this cannot happen. If he comes everything will be screwed."
Edward
" Come on guys you betrayed him, he deserves to be here that's where he belongs."
Nathan in anger walks towards Edward in high temper, " I'll fucking kill him you understand, i'll fuckin kill the bastard.
Nathan starts punching Edward in aggression, " And I will kill everyone who supports him. You got me junkie."
Nathan beats up Edward real bad and Bosco smiles watching Edward

getting beaten up.
At the same time at 'Dharavi' Peter, Michael and two guys were playing carrom board at Peter's brothel and the phone rings. Peter gets up saying, " I'll get it."
Michael
" It might be the Veron, she told me she will call back."
Peter
" Don't worry Mike, your girl never calls."
Peter gets towards the phone and picks up,"Speak "
Bosco replies," Peter is this you?"
Peter
" Yeah it's Peter. who are you ?"
Bosco
" Peter, it's Bosco. "
Peter
" Hey boss man, how are you? How's my cousin"
Bosco looks back at Edward and he was wiping blood from his face then he replies to Peter, "He is fine, we all are doing great. What about you guys?
Peter
" Never felt better in my life, The guy which you sent to me is a machine gun man. We made lot of money."
Bosco
" Listen to me very carefully that man cannot be trusted. He will ditch you and run away with the money."
Peter
" You mean this guy i don't think so?"
Bosco
" Yes he will, and he is headed back to Goa. His plan is to rob you and run from there. His girl just tipped me. He is a threat to everyone. Can you kill him there?

Peter watches back at Michael playing with friends and says," Are you sure, we are talking about the same guy?"

Bosco

"Yes I am talking about Michael."

Peter

" I don't think so he can betray anyone"

Bosco

"Trust me he will, we have known him for years. Gaining trust and betraying It's his nature. Tell me what you like more money or that guy. If you continue on this path you may land up in Jail or worst, tell me can you kill him?"

Peter again looks back at Michael

" It's not possible, but why you want to kill him?"

Bosco

" You have to do it Peter. Otherwise he will take control of everything. If you don't trust me you can ask him. He is having plans to come back to Goa."

Peter watches Michael playing and thinks for a while and says, " I can't kill him, but there is something i can do." and he hangs up the call and gets back on the game.

Michael while playing," Who was on the phone ?"

Peter answers jokingly," It was your girl, she was telling me come to Peter, come to me my love. I am very horny." Everyone laughs.

Michael gets annoyed," What the fuck man?"

Peter, "I am just kiddin, why don't you go and see her if you miss her so much?"

Michael

" I will be back to Goa soon. Miss that place a lot and I have to get rid of George's case as well."

Peter looks at him in suspicion and asks, " Why didn't you share your plans ?"

Michael

" It's not a plan or anything. It is something which needs to be done. One day I have to go home."

Peter remembers the words of Bosco that Michael will betray you and run with all the money. At that Moment Peter thinks Michael is a threat to him and his money. So he decides to finish him but not directly because the entire gang will turn against Peter. They continued their conversation while playing carrom.

Peter

"Well forget Goa for a while. We got a new gig, that was the phone call about but I am confused. I don't know if I should make a deal or not. "

Michael

"What is it?"

Peter

"No information of goods, we have to check it out."

Michael

" When can we check it?"

Peter

" Tomorrow night."

Michael

" Well then let's find out where this deal takes us." and he takes the striker in his hand and he strikes the queen to put it in the hole but the striker gets in the hole followed by the queen

Peter

" Michael looks like the queen got you in the hole."

Michael

" Yeah in real life too."

The night of Michael getting into a trap. Peter takes Michael to the slums in Dongri' a valley of violence. Peter stops his car in front of a slaughterhouse. They were waiting in their car to meet the contact and 5 minutes later an old crippled man comes near their car using crutches and bends down to look inside the car and puts a cigarette in his mouth and he asks Peter for a match box. Peter removes his lighter from his pocket and tries to light the cigarette. The crippled guy blows out the flame. Peter signs Michael that's the guy. The crippled guy starts walking away from them. Peters and Michael step out of their car and start following him. The guy went deep into the slums and stopped at a house with a green door and he knocked it. A huge man with a beard and big red eyes opened the door. The crippled guy signs the huge man that you got a visitor and he leaves. The huge man watches Peter and Michael and he gets back inside, leaving the door open. Michael and Peter looked at each other and they entered the house. As they entered they saw a group of people eating food in one giant plate on the floor and machine guns were next to them. The man who opened the door started checking them and both of them had guns. The huge guy takes their guns and tells them to enter a room pointing with his hand. Michael entered first and Peter was entering but the huge guy stopped Peter and said only one man can enter. So Peter told Michael to get inside, check the goods and come back soon, he will be waiting outside. And Michael agrees to enter alone.

When Michael enters he watches the entire room as empty, no goods but a long white bearded man who is speaking on a phone in some Arabic language. The man notices Michael has entered and he disconnects the phone. The bearded man starts speaking to Michael in foreign language . Michael had no clue what he was talking about. Then the man started removing carpet from the floor so Michael stepped aside. After removing the carpet he removed the wooden ply from the floor. As he removed the cover from his goods, Michael saw a metal cage and a few girls were tied down there. Michael gets shocked watching them. All this time he was standing in a cage. The girls were tied, their mouths were stuffed with cloth and they looked up at Michael, they couldn't speak but they were begging for their lives. Michael starts explaining to the bearded man that he is here for the guns, gold and drugs. The man didn't understand his language neither Michael understood his. And Police swooped in at that moment and grabbed Michael. It was a sudden attack and a rigid moment for Michael. Police handcuffed him and took him out of the house and as he was dragged out a press reporter took his picture. Police put him in the van and left the spot. Michael was fucked real good.

Michael was getting beaten up by the Police in the remand room. Police gave him third degree torture and to make him confess. After beating him for hours, the police put his head in the bucket of water and removed it in a few seconds and asked questions.

Police

" Tell me where did you bring the girls from?"

Michael

"You know better than me, Don't put this sheat on me."

Police

" You piece of sheat " and drop his head back in the water.

Police were desperate for his statement but Michael gave them nothing, for the sake of Peter and his Dharavi gang. But the law has ways to put a man behind bars. Michael was caught on the spot and the court sentenced him for 7 years in Arthur road Jail.

In Goa, Veronica watches Michael's picture in the newspaper and the article was about Cops raids the a place and caught Michael for human trafficking and was sentenced to Jail. She throws the newspaper away in the cabin and cheers, snorts, drinks, plays music on the jukebox and starts stripping joyfully in front of Nathan and Bosco. Their threesome started in front of Edward. Edward had marks on his face and was watching them cheer and fuck and he picks the news paper and reads the article. He was full of sorrow after reading about Michael landing in Jail but he couldn't do anything but watch the filth in front of him.

After the court's decision Michael was sent to Arthur road Jail in the Police van. On the road towards Jail, fear was eating him from inside. All the badass motherfuckers were locked up together in a joint and he has to live with them. It was the first time Michael will be in a prison. Police did their procedure to drop Michael into the Jail custody and sign the papers. And Michael's journey has begun in Jail. He was terrified and scared to death; it was something new for him. As he entered he was thunderstruck watching Rudy. And Rudy recognized Michael as one of Bosco 's men and he spoke to his cell mates, " Look what we have here? Bosco 's monkey in my Jail."

When the lights go off every prisoner was supposed to sleep in a big hall next to each other and Rudy used to run his show. He was the boss where everyone feared him. Michael got beat up in Jail several times by Rudy and his men at night, they even cut off his ponytail. Rudy didn't leave a single chance to torment him and Michael had no clue how he would survive the Jail. Michael's thoughts at that moment were like once you start getting fucked, it doesn't stops. There was the entire world out there and he had to land in a Jail where Rudy is. Michael's life was in danger and he asked a Jail mate how Rudy landed up in Mumbai prison. The Jail mate replied, "He was hospitalized after the gun fight in Goa. He was in coma for weeks and when he woke up first thing he did is raped the nurse and ran from there and reached Mumbai. After entering the city he looted a petrol pump and burned the place down while leaving, police caught him at a brothel.

Michael

" Same old Rudy, the devil himself threw him back from the hell."

Once Michael was eating food on the table and one of Rudy's men stabbed him in the back from behind. This incident panicked the environment and when Jailer asked Michael who stabbed him in the back? Michael knew but he didn't tell the Police . Jail mate asked Michael, " Why didn't you tell the Jailer that Rudy was behind the stabbing. "

Michael answered

"It won't make any difference, things will get worse after that. I just want to do my time and get the fuck out of here."

Back in Goa, Veronica is moving her stuff from the old house and Nathan is helping her. Being a neighbor Michael 's Mom noticed her and asked," Veronica where are you going? "

Veronica replies, " I am leaving this place."

Mom

" Then what about Michael ?"

Veronica

" What about him?"

Mom

" You leaving us just like that?"

Veronica

" Mike is long gone."

Mom

" Watch your mouth don't forget you are all because of Mike, he looked after you for so many years."

Veronica gets agitated,

" No one made me what i am, i am successful because of my talent and your son Mike looked after me so one day he could sell me."

Mom

" Do you have any idea what you are talking about?"

Veronica removes news paper from her purse and throws at her and says, " Look for yourself what your Mike has done."

Nathan speaks

" Yo mama Michael has turned bad. He killed George and moved to Mumbai . We helped him escape but there he kidnapped girls and started selling them. We cannot help him in this kind of mess. I am sorry, I never wanted you to know but I had to tell the truth."

Veronica takes Nathan away saying." Lets get the fuck out of this sheat hole" she picks her stuff and leaves.

Micheal's mother picks the newspaper and starts reading.

That night Mom couldn't sleep, the picture of Mike and the words from the news article went on revolving into her head and after that night the door of Michael's house was not opened for weeks, until one day Officer Alex Tusk visited the house on the complaint of neighbors of a bad smell. After checking the door he figured that the door was locked from inside. So he kicks and opens the door and the floor gets more fetid. Officer Alex Tusk puts a cloth on his mouth and enters, he finds Michael's Mom dead on her bed. Officer Alex calls in the casino from a pay phone and informs Bosco that Michael's Mom is dead. What should we do?

Bosco questions," What do you do to people who die on streets with no family?"

Alex Tusk

" We incinerate them in a machine."

Bosco

" Then what are you waiting for, and listen just check the house there might be some jewellery of her."

Alex

" Alright boss, got it."

Bosco keeps the phone and informs Nathan, Edward and Veronica in the club about death.

Veronica replies, " Finally the old bitch is gone."

Bosco

" You want to do a funeral."

Veronica

" Who will do more drama? I am fed up with it. let it be. I don't even live there anymore."

Edward is stoned and after hearing these words he says, "You guys are gonna burn in hell. You bitch and you pimps disgusts me every moment."

Back in Arthur road Jail Michael was eating food and one guy from behind places a finger at his back and says, "Give me what you got? Or you'll be dead."

Michael didn't turns behind and he recognized the voice, " Hey Peter it's good to see you here."

Peter

" Really?"

Michael turns

" nah! Not really. But what happened? How did you get caught? It's impossible for police to find your brothel.

Peter

" When you got in everyone from the gang got paranoid. They thought I set you up and I might do the same to them. When I was at the dock unloading weapons from a cargo ship some fucker tipped me out and got me here."

Michael

" Sheat happens."

Peter

" Well sheat happens, look what happened to you. Got fucked for no reason."

Michael

" Yeah."

Peter

" I am sorry Mike. I am sorry for that night, I just ran away watching Cops. It was a fuckin trap for both of us. I didn't have time to alert you. I was lucky to outrun the cops."

Michael

" But not lucky enough, you are still here."

They both start laughing.

Peter

" So how is life here?"

Michael

" Not bad."

Peter watches Mike bleeding from his back and Peter points at it," But the blood from your back gives me a different idea."

At night, Peter is sleeping and Rudy's guys grab him, and block his mouth with a cloth so he shouldn't scream and they drag him towards the bathroom. Rudy was waiting there. As the men arrive with Peter, Rudy removes his pants, " Bring the new fish here." The men brings Peter towards a wall and turns him and Rudy removes Peter's pants.

Michael enters there and pushes Rudy and Rudy falls down. Rudy watches Michael from the floor and said,

" I think you didn't had it enough yet."

Peter humming,"Mike Mike."

Michael breaks the bulb from the top and then it gets dark and he helps Peter escape. The bulb sound alerts everyone in the Jail. Police enter the spot with a torch. Rudy and his men get caught and Michael takes Peter towards the sleeping section.

Peter

"What the fuck is this?"

Michael

"Just keep quiet. and sleep. don't make a sound. The cops will come in and starts counting everyone again and if they find you awake you will be bashed up."

Peter hears prisoners getting beaten by the Cops in the bathroom and he closes his eyes hearing them.

In the morning, Peter, Michael and a Jail mate were talking about last night at the prison activity ground below a tree.

Peter

" What the fuck happened last night?"

Jail mate

" It happens every night, we have to save our own asses here. You were lucky Mike was there for you."

Peter

" We gotta look for a run from here. We are not safe here."

Michael

" There is no way you can escape from here. Consider this all the wrongs we did in our lives and never got caught. This is the punishment for our actions. We are just paying for our sins."

At that moment, one Police calls on Michael and informs that he has a visitor. Michael rushed towards the visitor's cell saying, " It might be my mother, guys I'll be back."

Michael comes near the visitors' cell and he watches George on the other side of the bars.

Michael

" George , is it you? What are you doing here?"

George

" I came to see you Mike"

Michael

" It's so good to see you George. Where have you been?"

George

" When you let me go that night. I got on a ferry which sailed till 'Colaba' Mumbai and started working in a small boat as a helper. I catch fish for a living. When I was a kid I always went fishing with my father and I never thought this experience would help me survive. I don't make any big bugs here, otherwise I would have got you out. I am so sorry."

Michael

" It's ok, George, there is one thing I need from you, please find a way to inform my gang that I am stuck here. They might help me out. Mom must have gone crazy looking out for me. I need to get out from here."

George

" I saw your article in the newspaper, and couldn't stop myself from coming here. Try to understand, what I want to tell you."

Michael

" Understand what?"

George

" This means they know about you and they are not coming for you."

Michael looks down in sorrow.

George

" For god sake Mike, when are you gonna learn, those 3 guys are homeless bastards. They want everything, what they see. They are like the vultures, they wait until you are dead and when you die, they fill their belly."

Michael

" I am worried about my Mom now."

George

" Your Mom is dead, she died in her house of a heart attack. For weeks her body was in the house. she didn't even had a proper funeral."

Michael in anger

" Where is Veronica? I told her to take care of my mom."

George nods his head no and walks away saying, " I will visit you again Mike." And he leaves.

Police take Michael away from the visitor's cell and he is shocked to hear about Mom. Michael enters inside the prisoners activity ground and his eyes get on Rudy. Michael starts walking towards him and Rudy is not aware of this situation and enters the gym. Michael passes by Peter.

Peter asks, " Hey Mike, how was your visit?"

Michael did not reply and kept walking towards the gym where Rudy went.

Peter asks the Jail mate

" What is wrong with him?"

Jail mate

" Looks like it was bad visit."

Michael gets inside the gym and finds Rudy doing the bench-press. Michael snatches a dumbbell from a guy who was working out and throws it at the guy's face who was helping Rudy with the bench-press. Immediately Rudy shacks the heavy weight and gets up. Michael picks a rod from the floor and hits on Rudy 's forehead, Rudy lies back on the bench holding his head in pain. Then Michael keeps on punching Rudy's face even after it's covered with blood. The guy who was helping Rudy ran from there watching Michael pounding Rudy. Police get informed by someone and they arrive at the spot whistling and watch Michael punching unconscious Rudy on the bench. Cops catch Michael and take him to the dark cell and beat him to death.

Back in Goa, officer Alex Tusk is getting his weekly payment from Bosco in his cabin. Bosco pays him to do his dirty work. At that moment Veronica is completely high on drugs and alcohol on a couch next to Nathan.

Officer Alex takes the money, counts it and says, " This is too less man, the work I've been doing for you is too much. I framed guy's for you, I even framed Michael . I protect you from everyone. I do all your dirty work wearing uniform."

Bosco

" That's why your getting paid."

Officer Alex

" But it's less."

Veronica snorts and speaks in arrogance," I think that's too much for you, that's the exact number you will get from here."

Officer Alex turns his face towards Veronica and asks Bosco, " When did this girl started getting involved in our business?"

Veronica stands up from the couch

" This girl? I am the boss's girl. I decide whether you are worthy or not. Any jackass in uniform can do the job."

Bosco and Nathan laughs

Alex

" What is this? Is this some kind of joke? It's not funny Bosco."

Nathan gets up and stops Veronica from talking and says do not interfere. Veronica doesn't listen and starts coming closer to Officer Alex like she is gonna pounce on him, "You are just a dog, do as we say and get paid. You want a raise lick my shoes, then maybe i'll think of it."

Nathan takes her away

" Come on we got to finish this dope, don't we?"

Officer Alex watches her and says, " Looks like the dope got her head." And before leaving he said , " Bosco next time call me when she is not around."

Veronica has become addicted to the substance and acts crazy. She is a complete mess.

Back in Mumbai prison, Michael was in a dark cell for many days, he didn't see sunlight for a long time. Cops get him out of the cell. As Michael comes out his eyes hurt from the light, his beard has grown and he became skinny and weak. Michael comes out towards the prison activity ground very slowly he can barely walk, the jail mate enters from his back and holds him and takes him towards the tree

and every prisoner is staring at them while they are walking.
Michael speaks in a soft voice
" What's happening?"
Jail mate
" You been in for a month, no one survived this long"
Michael
" Where the fuck is Rudy ?"
Jail mate
" Rudy is alive and landed up in city hospital, didn't came back yet."
Michael notices everyone are watching him and he asks to Jail mate," What are this guys looking at?"
Jail mate
" They are watching a man, who has some serious balls man."
Michael and Jail mate reach near the tree and they see Peter was already there.
Peter gets shocked watching Michael
" When did they release him?"
Jail mate
" Just now."
Peter and Jail mate help Michael to sit under the tree. One prisoner comes towards Michael and gives him a cigarette. Michael takes it and the prisoner lights it with a match box and he leaves.
Michael while smoking asks
" What is this all about?"
Jail mate replies, " Looks like you are the boss now."
Every prisoner starts gathering around Michael. As if some celebrity has arrived.
Back in Goa, George's wife and Officer Alex Tusk were having sex together at her house. He was lying on the bed and she was performing in a cowboy position.
George's wife while performing sex

" I want to finish that bitch. She took away all my dreams. You got to do something Officer."

Alex Tusk

" ohh !yes! yes!. Please don't bring this up now. just continue what you are doing."

After a few seconds Alex cums and George's wife gets up from him and lies on the bed next to him and officer Alex lights a cigarette.

George's wife

" Did you even hear me what i said?"

Alex Tusk

" Yeah, You don't have to do anything, she has become an addict. She is finished come by the casino and watch it yourself."

At the casino, the stage was set as usual and the crowd was waiting for Veronica to perform. Veronica enters the stage completely drunk and stands in front of the mic. The audience was aware that she was tripping on substance. The musicians starts playing and she starts singing. She was a disaster while performing, forgot the lines, coughed while singing and later she also puked on the stage. She just couldn't sing and the audience were watching each other's face wondering what the heck are they watching. Edward was laughing at a card counter watching her, "What is this sheat show?"

Nathan was having a drink in the cabin and Bosco comes running,"Nathan look at this sheat, she is doing on the stage."

Nathan and Bosco rush towards the stage and as her disaster song ends no one claps.

Veronica to the crowd

" You guys are supposed to clap assholes. What the fuck are you looking at? I said clap."

The audience keeps watching her and no one says a word.

Bosco tells Nathan to get her off the stage, everyone has seen enough. Nathan gets there and tries to take her out of the stage. She just snaps at him too. Veronica hears a clap and she looks in the audience, it was George 's wife.

George's wife loudly, "Clap, everyone just clap for this junkie," and everyone in the crowd starts clapping. No one has a clue what's going on.

Veronica shouts in mic pointing at George's wife, " You fuckin cunt."

The audience stops clapping and Nathan holds Veronica's hand but she tossed his hand away.

Veronica continues yelling, "You came here back you bitch. Security kicked her out, remember this is you slut, this is my place, this is my man, no one can take me away from this glam."

Nathan had enough of her and he just picks her up and takes her away from the stage. she is still abusing, while she is getting carried away and the crowd starts clapping, after getting rid of her. Edward is also laughing and clapping joyfully with the crowd. Nathan takes Veronica in the cabin and she keeps on hitting Nathan for lifting her from the stage. Nathan just drops her in the cabin.

Veronica in rage, "What the fuck is going on, this bitch came here again. Tell me Nathan, what the fuck are you gonna do next. kick me out like you did with Mike and bring her in.

Edward enters laughing and watches Veronica mad," That was quite a show."

Veronica screams at Edward, "Shut the fuck up asshole."

Edward continues laughing and Nathan also asks him to shut it up.

Edward

" Alright my bad."and he stops laughing.

Veronica gets up and comes closer to Nathan and starts wailing,

" Tell me, you are not gonna dump me Nathan, I am with you from the beginning. Wait, wait a second." she turns back and drinks from the bottle of whiskey and she removes her one piece dress and grabs Nathan's shirt and starts tearing it, "Lets have a fuck, come on, give

me some wild time." She starts forcing Nathan.
Bosco enters the cabin with chorus girls and they all get shocked watching her nude.
Veronica screams, "What the fuck are you looking at." Bosco in fear takes the girls out.
Veronica wailing again, "Nathan don't tell me you are leaving me for her. "
Nathan
" No i am not gonna leave you, it's just the drug problem."
Veronica replies
"What drug problem? She gets back on the table and snorts cocaine and says, " No, no more drugs. I'll stop everything. I swear, I have to get back on the top. I deserve that light, i deserve that stage."
Next night a new beautiful girl was singing on the stage of the casino. She sings and when the song gets over everyone claps and even Edward shouts loudly for the singer from the craps counter, " Bravo, bravo. " and returns back to the game he was playing and he picks the dice. The white haired guy is next to him. He is the same guy who was mugged by Edward at an Irish club and at present Edward is wearing his ring.
One player asks, "What happened to the old singer?"
Edward replies, " She went fuckin crazy, dope got her head."
Edward throws the dice and he loses. The croupier informs you loose. Edward and the white haired guy places the bet again. Edward kisses his ring and the guy notices it. When he watches the ring closely, he recognizes it. He knew it was his ring and he asks, " Where did you get this ring."
Edward
" This ring its my good luck." and picks the dice again and says, "Come on give me a six"
Edward throws the dice and he loses again.

Edward

" Come on this is cheating, this dice are loaded."

The croupier replies, " Sir this is your club."

Edward

"Ohh i forgot."

The same guy who asked about Veronica asks again where she is now. Edward replies to him that Nathan kicked her out of the house yesterday. The crowd next to him wanted to know why. Edward explained the drugs messed her head, after the last nights fuck up, Nathan took her home and they slept. In the middle of the night, Nathan just woke because of some odd smell like a dead rat. He looked around, it was nothing, then he checked his bed. It was Veronica who pooped in the bed and was lying all over it. Nathan just kicked her out and took the ruby which he gave her.

The same guy asks again, " But where did she go?"

Edward

" Why do you wanna know so much, do you want poop in you bed too?"

Everyone around the table starts laughing. Edward picks the dice again and says, "Come on, give me a 8." The croupier puts the tokens of Edward on 8 and the white haired guy also bets on 8 watching the ring.

Edward

" First you take a person in from the streets, you give them a good life, but that same person finds a way back to that street. People get what they deserve."

The white haired guy watches the ring and then at Edward's face and says, "Well I am with you, they all deserve the streets."

Edward throws the dice and the dice drops on table as number 7.

Same night, when the casino shuts down Bosco gets out with the chorus girls and Nathan with George's wife. They were about to get in their car and Veronica swooped, in a messed up state.

Veronica

" Stop! Where are you guys going? Don't fucking leave me."

Everyone continues getting in the car.

Nathan

" This bitch has gone crazy."

Veronica stops them and implores

" No, no, don't take them please. I am here Nathan. You know how sexy i am."

Nathan and Bosco laugh at her. Veronica catches Nathan's collar in frustration, "You bastard"

Nathan

" What the fuck?" He pushes her and she falls down, " Get the fuck out of here." and he gets in the car.

Fallen Veronica begs and weeps again, " Please don't go, at least give me some dope."

Nathan opens the car window and throws coins, "This is what you are worthy for." and the car leaves.

Veronica picks a stone, gets up and throws it at the car. But the car went in speed and it was out of range.

Veronica

" You asshole , you took me like a dog and left me on the street. Michael was much better than you fucks."

Back to Jail Michael shaved his beard except the mustache. He is walking in the Jail and everyone salutes him passing by. He sits in the dinners and prisoners bring him food. And now the tables have turned.

Veronica is out on the street looking for dope. She catches a peddler and asks for dope. Peddler replies he has some jabs.

Veronica

" I don't know, what is it?"

Peddler answers, " All drug are same."
Veronica agrees and starts searching for money or jewellery. The peddler figures she has no bug on her.

peddler

" No money, no stuff."

Veronica starts honey potting

" Come on, we can work it out."

Peddler leers for a few seconds and agrees to her offer. He takes Veronica to the same burned factory where Michael fell when he was a child. Peddler makes her sit on the floor next to him in a corner and jabs a dose of drug and she calms down. Then he unzips his pants, removes his cock out and drags her face on it, holding her neck. When he is done he watches Veronica unconscious on the floor. So the peddler gets up, cleans a table from the factory and lifts Veronica and keeps her on the table. And at the same moment, Michael is drinking and smoking in Jail with Peter and Jail mate. The prisoners just worship Micheal.

Back to burned factory, there is a long queue outside to fuck Veronica. Peddler is sending men inside, one at a time and taking money from them. After a few hours one guy comes out and informs that she is getting awake. Peddler stops the crowd from getting in and gives her one more insulin of drug and comes out saying the crowd, " Now you can have her, but one at a time."

Next day Bosco and Nathan were headed towards the casino in their car reading the article of Veronica in the newspaper. The article said that children found a dead singer in the burned factory while playing hide and seek.

Nathan

" This papers says she overdosed herself."

Bosco

" Yeah she never knew when to stop. I thought we might have to kill

her someday."
Nathan gets stupefied after listening to these words. Bosco replies, "What are you stressing for? More Veronica are gonna come and go. Don't forget We have to run this place."

Nathan

" But i am worried, this shouldn't come on us."

Bosco

" So why do you think I am paying Officer Alex. Relax man I got everything sorted," and the driver stops the car after reaching the casino.

Bosco

" This place is filled with broads. We can fish every night." and they enter inside the casino and get confused, the place is secluded. Not a single soul in the casino.

Bosco reacts," Where the fuck is everyone?"

Nathan

" It must be the junky."

Bosco and Nathan believed that Edward must be the reason behind this emptiness of the ambience. They sprint towards the cabin. As they enter they see Edward is hanged like Jesus on the wall and all his intestines are out of his belly. It was a horrible sight. Bishop and his bodyguards enter from their back. Bosco and Nathan turns back, hearing his footsteps and after watching Bishop they starts walking backwards inside the cabin in terror.

Bishop enters and sits on a chair and the white haired guy is next to him standing.

Bishop

" Three junkies grew up doing loot on the street and next they opened a card game club. Things were good but soon they started up a royal casino which has space for hundreds of men to play, Expensive gaming machine and even spacious enough to set a stage for performers. I wonder where the money came from? I guess i know where it came from."

Bosco and Nathan beg for their life together. Please don't kill them. They are sorry for what we have done. Forgive them for their mistake.

Bishop

"Forgive you, for what? I should thank you for such a wonderful place. You guy did a good investment."

Bosco

" Yes boss, the place is yours just don't kill us."

Bishop

" I give you 24 hours to start. If I catch you after that you will land up like your friend or maybe worse. Your time starts now."

Bosco and Nathan looks at each other and Bishop gives an evil smile and speaks in a very slow tone, "The clock is ticking, tick tock tick tock tick tock."

Nathan and Bosco make a run from there saving their lives. Darkness has fallen back in their lives. Both were terrified, helpless, lost everything they owned and had to leave Goa for good. They stopped by Bosco's house before leaving. Bosco is drinking and Nathan is pacing in the house. Suddenly Nathan stops and speaks, "How much time do we have?"

Bosco didn't care to answer. Nathan gets agitated," Is this the time to drink? Listen we lost the casino and we are about to lose our lives and you are sitting there and drinking."

Bosco

" Hey, we are in this together, don't crack on me like this. Just relax."

Nathan

" You must be insane. How can you be so calm? We lost everything."

Bosco

" No not yet, just grab all the money from the house and lets make a move from here."

Nathan

" Where?"

Bosco

" Mumbai, We got into a big fight, and we are going to need a weapon."

On a sunny afternoon. Michael , Peter and Jail mate talking to each other at the same spot below the tree.

Peter

" So what's next? "

Michael

" I'll settle down in Mumbai. Start a new life, maybe i'll go legit this time."

Peter

" So when will it be in 10 years? I won't do a single a day in this sheat hole."

Jail mate asks michael

" So you are not going back?"

Michael

" No, there is no in Goa for me. Mom's dead and it looks like Veron is with someone else, she left Mom too."

Peter

" I told you, she was no good."

A Cop enters and informs Michael that he has a visitor, Michael gets up and says, "It might be George , i'll be back in sometime." and he leaves with the Cop.

Jail mate

" I wonder, what will happen this time? his last visit was not that good."

Michael enters the visitor's cell and gets startled watching Bosco and Nathan on the other side of the bars. Michael was angry at them because they didn't show up when he was locked up and even when his mom was dead.

Michael

" Guys what brings you here now?"

Bosco

" Come on Mike we came to see you."

Michael

" My Mom rotted for a week in her house after her death. Where is Veron?"

Nathan

" Veron is dead too." and he starts crying and Michael gets more shocked. Nathan shows him the newspaper and says, "She died from overdose"

Bosco

" It's a lie , she was killed like Eddy and your Mom."

Michael

" By who?"

Bosco

" It was Bishop. He killed them both and took over the casino. We ran from there and next he is coming for you. There is a plan to kill you in Jail."

Michael

" Why me?"

Bosco

" He knows about the loot and wants to set an example, to show the world, what he do to the people, who rob him."

Michael looks down and starts thinking about what he should do next and Bosco speaks, "Its nothing in Goa for us now, we have to make a run."

Michael looks up.

" Running won't help."

Bosco

" So what can we do?"

Michael

" Release me and of my two of my friends, i think it's time for hell or high water."

Bosco smiles

" You will be out in few days, just give me your friends names."

At the same night Peter, Michael and Jail mate outside in the activity ground below the tree. Though prisoners were caged at night, Michael had his way to come out anytime he wanted. Michael tells them the story about the visit from Bosco and after listening Peter replies, " I don't trust that guy. I'd rather stay here. I will be alive."

Michael

" What is it about you and him? give me reason."

Peter

" You are the reason."

Michael

" What?"

Peter

" I haven't been completely honest with you."

Michael

" About what?"

Peter

" About me getting locked up. Our own Dharavi friends tipped me out."

Michael

" What i have to do with this?"

Peter

" Because I framed you. You are rotting here because of me. I was the rat, later the gang got paranoid and they tipped me out."

Michael just looks at him and keeps on listening.

Peter

" Yes Mike I betrayed you, Bosco told me to kill you but I didn't, I don't want you dead, I just got you in here.

Michael in agony

"But why?"

Peter

"Bosco poisoned my head that you are gonna betray me, take away the money and disappear."

Michael

" We pulled off many gigs together, have I ever been dishonest to you? You were a friend, you should have trusted me?"

Peter

" I am sorry Mike, I was too scared. I had no time to think, i did this for my safety"

Michael

"You have no idea what you have done."

Peter

" I will do as you say from now on, I will never betray you again. I am sorry Mike." and Peter leaves the spot. Jail mate and Michael are sitting there stunned. After few minutes of silence Jail mate said, " Just tell me, do you want him dead tonight." Michael watches his face and again looks in front of him and he is drowned in his thoughts. After a massive struggle, Bosco finds a way to release the prisoners. And in a sunny afternoon Michael comes out of the prison gate with Peter and Jail mate, he sees Bosco and Nathan waiting for them in his car. Michael, Peter and Jail mate enter the car and settle at the back seat. The First thing which Nathan asked is, "Where to go now Mike?"

Michael

" Just drive."

Nathan starts driving

Bosco lights a cigarette in the front seat and turns back and gives it to Peter and says " I am sorry for your loss."

Peter

"What loss?"

Bosco

"Mike didn't tell you about Eddy. "

Peter

" He did but Eddy was a piece of sheat anyways."

Michael keeps on showing Nathan the way towards slums in Dharavi and Nathan drives till there without a question. As they reached the spot Michael stepped out of his car and started walking inside the small lanes in the slum and everyone was following him. Bosco gets scared watching the place, it was too populated and congested. He even asked Michael, " Are you planning to kill me, look i am the one, who got you out." Michael didn't care to reply, he just went on walking into the slum. As Michael reached the brothel, the Dharavi gang hugged him and were happy to see him and after watching Peter they just couldn't resist his sight there. The Dharavi gang was about to kill him but Michael stopped them and said, " Forget what he did and focus on what we are going to do, we got a bigger fish to fry." The Dharavi gang figured from his words that there is a new gig. The gang asked, "Who are we against?" Michael replied, "We are against an army." The gang started packing the machine guns, bullet magazines and grenades. Bosco and Nathan were stunned watching the amount of guns being packed. Michael selects 8 of his friends from the Dharavi gang to come with him. And they all came outside the slums with loaded bags of guns. As they come out, Michael tells them to load the guns in 4 cars and they do as he said. Everyone just gets in the car without asking.

Next Michael with his gang heads towards Colaba, at the fish dock where George is working. Michael finds George was removing fish from the nets. Michael stops the gang at a distance and he meets him alone. George gets happy watching Michael out of the prison. After a few Moments George notices Michael is not alone. Nathan, Bosco and more men are standing watching them. George asks, " What is this all about?"

Michael

" It's about getting our lives back."

Without any more questions, George starts walking with Michael towards the car. Nathan apologizes to George and George replies, " Let's put the past behind us and do what we got to do."

Next Michael with the entire gang enters the city hospital. He watches there was a Cop outside a ward. Michael knew, when any prisoner is hospitalized a Cop is always there to keep an eye on him. Michael starts entering the ward. Cop tries to stop him but the Dharavi gang points a gun at him so he shouldn't make any moves. And the cop in fear stopped right there and didn't move a muscle. Michael gets inside Rudy's ward, he was alone and his hands were cuffed on the bed's edge's metal pipe.

Rudy

" You got some nerve coming here." and tries to remove his handcuffs in aggression.

Michael asks

" You want out or you want to rot back in Jail?"

After a few minutes of conversation. Michael comes out of the hospital with Rudy. Rudy was in his hospital gown and met Bosco.

Bosco in fear

" No hard feelings Rudy . I got you out."

Rudy smiles sarcastically and says, "Yeah, no hard feelings."

It was night when Michael informed Bosco that we needed someone from the police. There will be a check post when we enter Goa. Bosco replies, "don't worry, i'll get it covered." Bosco calls from the nearest payphone to officer Alex Tusk's house and Alex was sleeping with George's wife. The phone rings and George's wife wakes Alex to get the phone. Alex picks up the phone when it rings a second time. Bosco informs that he is headed towards Goa from Mumbai with Michael and a few of his friends and he wants to pass the check post. Officer Alex replies, it will be done. After this phone call, the entire gang heads towards Goa.

After 12 hours of nonstop drive Michael and his gang stopped at Goa check post and Officer Alex was there waiting for them.

Michael was in his car and Alex bent down to talk to him," It's good to see you Mike. I am sorry for everything, it was nothing personal, don't hold any grudges. "

Michael

" Whatever is done is done. I have forgotten everything and it's time for you too."

Alex

" You are absolutely right Mike, i am with you"

Alex stands up straight after speaking with Michael and tells his fellow officers to let these cars enter. Michael passes from the check post. Michael and his gang stop at the graveyard and start removing the guns from the trunk of the cars. It was noon, when everyone was with a machine gun, extra bullets, magazines and grenades. The entire gang gets in their cars with guns in their hands and starts driving towards the Bishop's place at speed.

Bishop's castle had a big gate. Michael drives his car in speed towards the gate and dashed his car on the gate. The gate broke and the way to enter the castle was unlocked. The gang rushed inside with their cars.

Bishop had his own army, His guys started shooting at the cars entering the premises. Michael's gang comes out of their cars and starts shooting at them back. Bishop was at his dining table, eating food with his family and they heard the gunshots. The family panics. The Bishop informs his family to take the secret door underground and leave the place and he decides to face the fire. His family, wife, children and his grandchildren implored to come with them. Bishop answers, " I always knew from the beginning, this day will come, I guess, today is that day. "

Bishop makes his family run from the castle through the secret door and enters into a room and keeps his door open for his enemies and gets seated on a chair and starts drinking wine. He didn't care what's coming.

Outside the castle, every guy from Michael's gang is shooting at Bishop's army except Michael. It was the reign of bullets. The gang killed all the Bishop's men, who were guarding the castle outside. Michael takes a machine gun, and starts entering the castle. Michael is walking and his gang is shooting, whoever is coming in his way. Once even Michael gets shot on his shoulder but he didn't shoot back, his guys took down the man who shot Michael. The entire bishop's men were killed by Michael's gang. Michael reaches the room where Bishop was sitting and drinking wine. Michael enters alone and locks the door from inside and starts walking towards Bishop with a machine in his hand.

Bishop watching Michael says, " So you are the one, who is gonna be the new boss, I congratulate you."

Michael asks in grieve

" Why my Mom and Veron?"

Bishop

" I don't even know, who the fuck are you?"

Michael looks at him in confusion.

Bishop

" We'll do it, what you came here for?"

Michael lifts his gun and points at him. The gang outside the room hears the sound of shots fired and assumes that Michael has killed Bishop. After this massive gunfight, everyone comes out of the castle. Michael meets Bosco and Nathan. Bosco asks, " Is he dead?"

Michael replies

" Yes he is. "

Bosco

" Then it's time for a celebration. Let's grab a drink at our old place?"

Michael

" No i have to be somewhere."

Bosco

" Are you sure?"

Michael

" yeah, I am damn sure."

Bosco

" Alright Mike, you are the boss."

Bosco gets in a car. Nathan hugs Michael, thanks him and gets in the Bosco 's car. Michael watches them go with Peter, Rudy, George, Jail mate and Dharavi guys.

Michael tells everyone to get in the car before the cops drop in. Everyone gets in the car and starts following Michael's car. Jail mate gives a sharp knife to Rudy in the car and Rudy just takes it without questioning. Peter and George are loading their machine guns in the car.

Nathan asked Bosco in the car, "how does it feel when you call a small kid boss?"

Bosco replied, " it hurts but what can we do? He is the boss but not for long, he is going back to prison because his trafficking case is going to start again."

Nathan laughingly, "ahhh, bosco you got it all covered up."

Bosco answers, " well you got to fix some people if you want to see yourself as the boss."

Bosco drops Nathan at George's house and leaves towards the souls casino. Nathan rings the doorbell and George's wife opens the door and he enters the house kissing her. Bosco entered his casino, but there was no one around. Bosco plays the opera in the music system, sits near the bar counter, makes a drink for him and relaxes.

At sunset, Michael and his gang were in their cars. First Michael drops Rudy in front of the casino. Rudy bows in front of Michael and starts walking towards the casino, then he drops Peter near the hookers standing on the street, and then George in front of George's house. Then Michael takes the remaining gang to a cake shop and buys pastries for everyone and he takes two of them packed for himself. Michael with his gang heads back towards his old house in Goa. He takes the pastry box and asks everyone to stay down till he comes back, he has something important to do. Michael enters his house and sheds a tear looking around. Then he cleans the dining table, chair and he wipes his Mother's picture and keeps it on the table in front of him and lights a candle at the center of the table. Next Michael opens the pastry box and he keeps one piece in front of his Mother's picture and the second one, he starts eating very slowly.

While he was eating the cake. Officer Alex was patrolling on the road and he stopped in front of a hooker standing by her car. It looked as if her car had stopped and Alex asked her about the problem. she pointed at the flat tyre. Alex stepped out of his Police car and asked if there was a spare tire? She replied that there is one in the trunk. Alex walks near the trunk and opens it facing the girl

Alex

" I'll fix it for you, don't worry."

As he looks down in the trunk. Peter was inside the trunk and shot him with a machine gun.

Bosco was at his casino, listening to music and drinking scotch. Rudy comes from behind and cuts his throat with the knife.

Nathan was fucking George's wife and George enters from his behind very quietly and puts gun in the Nathan ass and shoots. George keeps on shooting until Nathan and his wife die.

At the same time Michael finishes his cake, gets up from the chair, kisses his Mother's picture, keeps back in front of the candle and leaves the house.

A house with a big swimming pool and from the balcony Bishop was watching his family members by the pool. Children were playing and others were enjoying their time there. His Butler comes with a huge bag of money.

Butler

" Sir your package."

Bishop

" Just leave it there, i'll keep it in the vault."

Butler

" Sir the phone call."

Bishop looks at the butler.

Butler replies " It's him."

Bishop takes the phone.

Bishop, " Yes Michael "

Michael is sitting in his chair in front of Peter and Jail mate in the souls casino cabin.

Michael

" Did you get your package?"

Bishop

" Yes i did."

Michael

" You will get your cut every week. The safety of you and your family is my responsibility. I have no quarrels with you but" ..... Michael stops speaking and hangs up the call.

Bishop gives the phone to Butler.

Bishop

" What happened about the Rudy's meeting."

Butler answers

" Our guys found him dead on our yacht . "

Bishop smiles.

"He has no quarrels with me but he is the boss."

Butler

"I didn't get you sir."

Butler left from there after no reply and Bishop continued looking at the pool at his family.

Back in the casino, Michael is watching the red phone on his desk and the blood is reaching the phone very slowly and he is hearing voices of Veronica from his childhood "You be the boss man. You have to be the boss man or you are not welcome at my house. Mike get inside, see what they are doing, if you wont go, I will never speak to you again." and the blood was about to reach the phone so Michael moves the phone away and he looks at Jail mate and Peter. Peter was dead and his head was on the table and it was his blood on the desk. Mike gets up from his chair, picks up the jacket hanging behind his chair and starts walking outside his cabin, wearing the jacket. Jail mate follows him. One guy wearing gloves with a big plastic bag enters his cabin. George was standing outside his cabin. As Michael walks, George also starts following him. Michael enters the casino play section, everyone salutes him. The Dharavi gang also starts following him. Michael suddenly stops hearing the girl on the stage. She was singing the 'Rapture' song. Michael turned and watched the stage. The singer continued singing and smiled watching him. Michael looked back at his guys for a second and no one had a clue why he suddenly stopped. Then he continued walking on his path outside the club and the entire gang followed him. Everyone gets in their cars to visit every night club Michael owns in Goa.

Contents

9 798887 041896

Printed by Libri Plureos GmbH in Hamburg, Germany